Bjornstjerne Bjornson

The Bridal March and One Day

Bjornstjerne Bjornson

The Bridal March and One Day

1st Edition | ISBN: 978-3-75236-532-0

Place of Publication: Frankfurt am Main, Germany

Year of Publication: 2020

Outlook Verlag GmbH, Germany.

Reproduction of the original.

THE BRIDAL MARCH

&

ONE DAY

BY

BJÖRNSTJERNE BJÖRNSON

THE BRIDAL MARCH

THERE lived last century, in one of the high-lying inland valleys of Norway, a fiddler, who has become in some degree a legendary personage. Of the tunes and marches ascribed to him, some are said to have been inspired by the Trolls, one he heard from the devil himself, another he made to save his life, &c., &c. But the most famous of all is a Bridal March; and *its* story does not end with the story of his life.

Fiddler Ole Haugen was a poor cottar high among the mountains. He had a daughter, Aslaug, who had inherited his cleverness. Though she could not play his fiddle, there was music in everything she did—in her talk, her singing, her walk, her dancing.

At the great farm of Tingvold, down in the valley, a young man had come home from his travels. He was the third son of the rich peasant owner, but his two elder brothers had been drowned in a flood, so the farm was to come to him. He met Aslaug at a wedding and fell in love with her. In those days it was an unheard-of thing that a well-to-do peasant of old family should court a girl of Aslaug's class. But this young fellow had been long away, and he let his parents know that he had made enough out in the world to live upon, and that if he could not have what he wanted at home, he would let the farm go. It was prophesied that this indifference to the claims of family and property would bring its own punishment. Some said that Ole Haugen had brought it about, by means only darkly hinted at.

So much is certain, that while the conflict between the young man and his parents was going on, Haugen was in the best of spirits. When the battle was over, he said that he had already made them a Bridal March, one that would never go out of the family of Tingvold—but woe to the girl, he added, whom it did not play to church as happy a bride as the cottar's daughter, Aslaug Haugen! And here again people talked of the influence of some mysterious evil power.

So runs the story. It is a fact that to this day the people of that mountain district have a peculiar gift of music and song, which then must have been greater still. Such a thing is not kept up without some one caring for and adding to the original treasure, and Ole Haugen was the man who did it in his time.

Tradition goes on to tell that just as Ole Haugen's Bridal March was the merriest ever heard, so the bridal pair that it played to church, that were met by it again as they came from the altar, and that drove home with its strain in their ears, were the happiest couple that had ever been seen. And though the race of Tingvold had always been a handsome race, and after this were handsomer than ever, it is maintained that none, before or after, could equal this particular couple.

With Ole Haugen legend ends, and now history begins. Ole's bridal march kept its place in the house of Tingvold. It was sung, and hummed, and whistled, and fiddled, in the house and in the stable, in the field and on the mountain-side. The only child born of the marriage, little Astrid, was rocked and sung to sleep with it by mother, by father, and by servants, and it was one of the first things she herself learned. There was music in the race, and this bright little one had her full share of it, and soon could hum her parent's triumphal march, the talisman of her family, in quite a masterly way.

It was hardly to be wondered at that when she grew up, she too wished to choose her lover. Many came to woo, but at the age of twenty-three the rich and gifted girl was still single. The reason came out at last. In the house lived a quick-witted youth, whom Aslaug had taken in out of pity. He went by the name of the tramp or gipsy, though he was neither. But Aslaug was ready enough to call him so when she heard that Astrid and he were betrothed. They had pledged faith to each other in all secrecy out on the hill pastures, and had sung the bridal march together, she on the height, he answering from below.

The lad was sent away at once. No one could now show more pride of race than Aslaug, the poor cottar's daughter. Astrid's father called to mind what was prophesied when he broke the tradition of his family. Had it now come to a husband being taken in from the wayside? Where would it end? And the neighbours said much the same.

"The tramp," Knut by name, soon became well known to every one, as he took to dealing in cattle on his own account. He was the first in that part of the country to do it to any extent, and his enterprise had begun to benefit the whole district, raising prices, and bringing in capital. But he was apt to bring drinking bouts, and often fighting, in his train; and this was all that people talked of as yet; they had not begun to understand his capabilities as a business man.

Astrid was determined, and she was twenty-three, and her parents came to see that either the farm must go out of the family or Knut must come into it; through their own marriage they had lost the moral authority that might have stood them in good stead now. So Astrid had her way. One fine day the handsome, merry Knut drove with her to church. The strains of the family bridal march, her grandfather's masterpiece, were wafted back over the great procession, and the two seemed to be sitting humming it quietly, and very happy they looked. And every one wondered how the parents looked so happy

3

too, for they had opposed the marriage long and obstinately.

After the wedding Knut took over the farm, and the old people retired on their allowance. It was such a liberal one that people could not understand how Knut and Astrid were able to afford it; for though the farm was the largest in the district, it was not well-cultivated. But this was not all. Three times the number of workpeople were taken on, and everything was started in a new way, with an outlay unheard of in these parts. Certain ruin was foretold. But "the tramp"—for his nickname had stuck to him—was as merry as ever, and seemed to have infected Astrid with his humour. The quiet, gentle girl became the lively, buxom wife. Her parents were satisfied. At last people began to understand that Knut had brought to Tingvold what no one had had there before, working capital! And along with it he had brought the experience gained in trading, and a gift of handling commodities and money, and of keeping servants willing and happy.

In twelve years one would hardly have known Tingvold again. House and outbuildings were different; there were three times as many workpeople, they were three times as well off, and Knut himself, in his broadcloth coat, sat in the evenings and smoked his meerschaum pipe and drank his glass of toddy with the Captain and the Pastor and the Bailiff. To Astrid he was the cleverest and best man in the world, and she was fond of telling how in his young days he had fought and drunk just to get himself talked about, and to frighten her; "for he was so cunning!"

She followed him in everything except in leaving off peasant dress and customs; to these she always kept. Knut did not interfere with other people's ways, so this caused no trouble between them. He lived with his "set," and his wife saw to their entertainment, which was, however, modest enough, for he was too prudent a man to make unnecessary show or outlay of any kind. Some said that he gained more by the card-playing, and by the popularity this mode of life won for him, than all he laid out upon it, but this was probably pure malevolence.

They had several children, but the only one whose history concerns us is the eldest son, Endrid, who was to inherit the farm and carry on the honour of the house. He had all the good looks of his race, but not much in the way of brains, as is often the case with children of specially active-minded parents. His father soon observed this, and tried to make up for it by giving him a very good education. A tutor was brought into the house for the children, and when Endrid grew up he was sent to one of the agricultural training schools that were now beginning to flourish in Norway, and after that to finish off in town. He came home again a quiet young fellow, with a rather over-burdened brain and fewer town ways than his father had hoped for. But Endrid was a slow-witted youth.

The Pastor and the Captain, both with large families of daughters, had their eye on him. But if this was the reason of the increased attention they paid to Knut, they made a great mistake; the idea of a marriage between his son and a poor pastor's or captain's daughter, with no training to fit her for a rich farmer's wife, was so ridiculous to him that he did not even think it necessary to warn Endrid. And indeed no warning was needed, for the lad saw as well as his father that, though there was no need for his bringing more wealth into the family through his marriage, it would be of advantage if he could again connect it with one of equal birth and position. But, as ill-luck would have it, he was but an awkward wooer. The worst of it was that he began to get the name of being a fortune-hunter; and when once a young man gets this reputation, the peasants fight shy of him. Endrid soon noticed this himself; for though he was not particularly quick, to make up for it he was very sensitive. He saw that it did not improve his position that he was dressed like a townsman, and "had learning," as the country people said. The boy was sound at heart, and the result of the slights he met with was that by degrees he left off his town dress and town speech, and began to work on his father's great farm as a simple labourer. His father understood—he had begun to understand before the lad did—and he told his wife to take no notice. So they said nothing about marriage, nor about the change in Endrid's ways; only his father was more and more friendly to him, and consulted him in everything connected with the farm and with his other trade, and at last gave the management of the farm altogether into his hands. And of this they never needed to repent.

So the time passed till Endrid was thirty-one. He had been steadily adding to his father's wealth and to his own experience and independence; but had never made the smallest attempt at courtship; had not looked at a girl, either in their own district or elsewhere. And now his parents were beginning to fear that he had given up thoughts of it altogether. But this was not the case.

On a neighbouring farm lived in good circumstances another well-descended peasant family, that had at different times intermarried with the race of Tingvold. A girl was growing up there whom Endrid had been fond of since she was a little child; no doubt he had quietly set his heart on her, for only six months after her confirmation he spoke. She was seventeen then and he thirty-one. Randi, that was the girl's name, did not know at first what to answer; she consulted her parents, but they said she must decide for herself. He was a good man, and from a worldly point of view she could not make a better match, but the difference in their ages was great, and she must know herself if she had the courage to undertake the new duties and cares that would come upon her as mistress of the large farm. The girl felt that her parents would rather have her say Yes than No, but she was really afraid. She went to his mother, whom she had always liked, and found to her surprise that she knew nothing. But the mother was so delighted with the idea that with all her might she urged Randi to accept him. "I'll help you," she said. "Father will want no allowance from the farm. He has all he needs, and he doesn't wish his children to be longing for his death. Things will be divided at once, and the little that we keep to live on will be divided too when we are gone. So you see there will be no trouble with us." Yes, Randi knew all along that Knut and Astrid were kind and nice. "And the boy," said Astrid, "is good and thoughtful about everything." Yes, Randi had felt that too; she was not afraid but that she would get on with him—if she were only capable enough herself!

A few days later everything was settled. Endrid was happy, and so were his parents; for this was a much respected family that he was marrying into, and the girl was both nice-looking and clever; there was not a better match for him in the district. The parents on both sides consulted together, and settled that the wedding should be just before harvest, as there was nothing to wait for.

The neighbourhood generally did not look on the engagement in the same light as the parties concerned. It was said that the pretty young girl had "sold herself." She was so young that she hardly knew what marriage was, and the sly Knut had pushed forward his son before any other lovers had the chance. Something of this came to Randi's ears, but Endrid was so loving to her, and in such a quiet, almost humble way, that she would not break off with him; only it made her a little cool. Both his and her parents heard what was said, but took no notice.

Perhaps just because of this talk they determined to hold the wedding in great style, and this, for the same reason, was not unacceptable to Randi. Knut's friends, the Pastor, the Captain, and the Bailiff, with their large families, were to be among the guests, and some of them were to accompany the pair to church. On their account Knut wanted to dispense with the fiddlers—it was too old-fashioned and peasant-like. But Astrid insisted that they must be played to church and home again with the Bridal March of her race. It had made her and her husband so happy; they could not but wish to hear it again on their dear children's great festival day. There was not much sentiment about Knut; but he let his wife have her way. The bride's parents got a hint that they might engage the fiddlers, who were asked to play the old March, the family Bridal March, that had lain quiet now for a time, because this generation had worked without song.

But alas! on the wedding day the rain poured hard. The players had to wrap up their fiddles as soon as they had played the bridal party away from the farm, and they did not take them out again till they came within sound of the church-bells. Then a boy had to stand up at the back of the cart and hold an umbrella over them, and below it they sat huddled together and sawed away. The March did not sound like itself in such weather, naturally enough, nor was it a very merry-looking bridal procession that followed. The bridegroom sat with the high bridegroom's hat between his legs and a sou'-wester on his head; he had on a great fur coat, and he held an umbrella over the bride, who, with one shawl on the top of another, to protect the bridal crown and the rest of her finery, looked more like a wet hayrick than a human being. On they came, carriage after carriage, the men dripping, the women hidden away under their wrappings. It looked like a sort of bewitched procession, in which one could not recognise a single face; for there was not a face to be seen, nothing but huddled-up heaps of wool or fur. A laugh broke out among the specially large crowd gathered at the church on account of the great wedding. At first it was stifled, but it grew louder with each carriage that drove up. At the large house where the procession was to alight and the dresses were to be arranged a little for going into church, a hay-cart had been drawn out of the way, into the corner formed by the porch. Mounted on it stood a pedlar, a joking fellow, Aslak by name. Just as the bride was lifted down he called: "Devil take me if Ole Haugen's Bridal March is any good to-day!"

He said no more, but that was plenty. The crowd laughed, and though many of them tried not to let it be seen that they were laughing, it was clearly felt what all were thinking and trying to hide.

When they took off the bride's shawls they saw that she was as white as a sheet. She began to cry, tried to laugh, cried again—and then all at once the feeling came over her that she could not go into the church. Amidst great excitement she was laid on a bed in a quiet room, for such a violent fit of crying had seized her that they were much alarmed. Her good parents stood beside the bed, and when she begged them to let her go back, they said that she might do just as she liked. Then her eyes fell on Endrid. Any one so utterly miserable and helpless she had never seen before; and beside him stood his mother, silent and motionless, with the tears running down her face and her eyes fixed on Randi's. Then Randi raised herself on her elbow and looked straight in front of her for a little, still sobbing after the fit of crying. "No, no,!" she said, "I'm going to church." Once more she lay back and cried for a little, and then she got up. She said that she would have no more music, so the fiddlers were dismissed—and the story did not lose in their telling when they got among the crowd.

It was a mournful bridal procession that now moved on towards the church.

The rain allowed of the bride and bridegroom hiding their faces from the curiosity of the onlookers till they got inside; but they felt that they were running the gauntlet, and they felt too that their own friends were annoyed at being laughed at as part of such a foolish procession.

The grave of the famous fiddler, Ole Haugen, lay close by the church-door. Without saying much about it, the family had always tended it, and a new head-board had been put up when the old one had rotted away below. The upper part of it was in the shape of a wheel, as Ole himself had desired. The grave was in a sunny spot, and was thickly overgrown with wild flowers. Every churchgoer that had ever stood by it had heard from some one or other how a botanist in government pay, making a collection of the plants and flowers of the valley and the mountains round about, had found flowers on that grave that did not grow anywhere else in the neighbourhood. And the peasants, who as a rule cared little about what they called "weeds," took pride in these particular ones—a pride mixed with curiosity and even awe. Some of the flowers were remarkably beautiful. But as the bridal pair passed the grave, Endrid, who was holding Randi's hand, felt that she shivered; immediately she began to cry again, walked crying into the church, and was led crying to her place. No bride within the memory of man had made such an entrance into that church.

She felt as she sat there that all this was helping to confirm the report that she had been sold. The thought of the shame she was bringing on her parents made her turn cold, and for a little she was able to stop crying. But at the altar she was moved again by some word of the priest's, and immediately the thought of all she had gone through that day came over her; and for the moment she had the feeling that never, no, never again, could she look people in the face, and least of all her own father and mother.

Things got no better as the day went on. She was not able to sit with the guests at the dinner-table; in the evening she was half coaxed, half forced to appear at supper, but she spoiled every one's pleasure, and had to be taken away to bed. The wedding festivities, that were to have gone on for several days, ended that evening. It was given out that the bride was ill.

Though neither those who said this nor those who heard it believed it, it was only too true. She was really ill, and she did not soon recover. One consequence of this was that their first child was sickly. The parents were not the less devoted to it from understanding that they themselves were to a certain extent the cause of its suffering. They never left that child. They never went to church, for they had got shy of people. For two years God gave them the joy of the child, and then He took it from them.

The first thought that struck them after this blow was that they had been too fond of their child. That was why they had lost it. So, when another came, it seemed as if neither of them dared to show their love for it. But this little one, though it too was sickly at first, grew stronger, and was so sweet and bright that they could not restrain their feelings. A new, pure happiness had come to them; they could almost forget all that had happened. When this child was two years old, God took it too.

Some people seem to be chosen out by sorrow. They are the very people that seem to us to need it least, but at the same time they are those that are best fitted to bear trials and yet to keep their faith. These two had early sought God together; after this they lived as it were in His presence. The life at Tingvold had long been a quiet one; now the house was like a church before the priest comes in. The work went on perfectly steadily, but at intervals during the day Endrid and Randi worshipped together, communing with those "on the other side." It made no change in their habits that Randi, soon after their last loss, had a little daughter. The children that were dead were boys, and this made them not care so much for a girl. Besides they did not know if they were to be allowed to keep her. But the health and happiness that the mother had enjoyed up to the time of the death of the last little boy, had benefited this child, who soon showed herself to be a bright little girl, with her mother's pretty face. The two lonely people again felt the temptation to be hopeful and happy in their child; but the fateful two years were not over, and they dared not. As the time drew near, they felt as if they had only been allowed a respite.

Knut and Astrid kept a good deal to themselves. The way in which the young people had taken things did not allow of much sympathy or consolation being offered them. Besides, Knut was too lively and worldly-minded to sit long in a house of mourning or to be always coming in upon a prayer meeting. He moved to a small farm that he had bought and let, but now took back into his own hands. There he arranged everything so comfortably and nicely for his dear Astrid, that people whose intention it was to go to Tingvold, rather stayed and laughed with him than went on to cry with his children.

One day when Astrid was in her daughter-in-law's house, she noticed how little Mildrid went about quite alone; it seemed as if her mother hardly dared to touch her. When the father came in, she saw the same mournful sort of reserve towards his own, only child. She concealed her thoughts, but when she got home to her own dear Knut, she told him how things stood at Tingvold, and added: "Our place is there now. Little Mildrid needs some one that dares to love her; pretty, sweet little child that she is!" Knut was infected by her eagerness, and the two old people packed up and went home.

Mildrid was now much with her grandparents, and they taught her parents to love her. When she was five years old her mother had another daughter, who was called Beret; and after this Mildrid lived almost altogether with the old people. The anxious parents began once more to feel as if there might yet be pleasure for them in life, and a change in the popular feeling towards them helped them.

After the loss of the second child, though there were often the traces of tears on their faces, no one had ever seen them weep—their grief was silent. There was no changing of servants at Tingvold, that was one result of the peaceful, God-fearing life there; nothing but praise of master and mistress was ever heard. They themselves knew this, and it gave them a feeling of comfort and security. Relations and friends began to visit them again; and went on doing so, even though the Tingvold people made no return.

But they had not been at church since their wedding-day! They partook of the Communion at home, and held worship there. But when the second girl was born, they were so desirous to be her godparents themselves that they made up their minds to venture. They stood together at their children's graves; they passed Ole Haugen's without word or movement; the whole congregation showed them respect. But they continued to keep themselves very much to themselves, and a pious peace rested over their house.

One day in her grandmother's house little Mildrid was heard singing the Bridal March. Old Astrid stopped her work in a fright, and asked her where in the world she had learned that. The child answered: "From you, grandmother." Knut, who was sitting in the house, laughed heartily, for he knew that Astrid had a habit of humming it when she sat at work. But they both said to little Mildrid that she must never sing it when her parents were within hearing. Like a child, she asked "Why?" But to this question she got no answer. One evening she heard the new herd-boy singing it as he was cutting wood. She told her grandmother, who had heard it too. All grandmother said was: "He'll not grow old here!"—and sure enough he had to go next day. No reason was given; he got his wages and was sent about his business. Mildrid was so excited about this, that grandmother had to try to tell her the story of the Bridal March. The little eight year old girl understood it well enough, and what she did not understand then became clear to her later. It had an influence on her child-life, and especially on her conduct towards her parents, that nothing else had or could have had.

She had always noticed that they liked quietness. It was no hardship to her to please them in this; they were so gentle, and talked so much and so sweetly to her of the children's great Friend in heaven, that it cast a sort of charm over the whole house. The story of the Bridal March affected her deeply, and gave her an understanding of all that they had gone through. She carefully avoided recalling to them any painful memories, and showed them the tenderest affection, sharing with them their love of God, their truthfulness, their quietness, their industry. And she taught Beret to do the same.

In their grandfather's house the life that had to be suppressed at home got leave to expand. Here there was singing and dancing and play and story-telling. So the sisters' young days passed between devotion to their melancholy parents in the quiet house, and the glad life they were allowed to take part in at their grandfather's. The families lived in perfect understanding. It was the parents who told them to go to the old people and enjoy themselves, and the old people who told them to go back again, "and be sure to be good girls."

When a girl between the age of twelve and sixteen takes a sister between seven and eleven into her full confidence, the confidence is rewarded by great devotion. But the little one is apt to become too old for her years. This happened with Beret, while Mildrid only gained by being forbearing and kind and sympathetic—and she made her parents and grandparents happy.

There is no more to tell till Mildrid was in her fifteenth year; then old Knut died, suddenly and easily. There seemed almost no time between the day when he sat joking in the chimney-corner and the day when he lay in his coffin.

After this, grandmother's greatest pleasure was to have Mildrid sitting on a stool at her feet, as she had done ever since she was a little child, and to tell her stories about Knut, or else to get her to hum the Bridal March. As Astrid sat listening to it, she saw Knut's handsome dark head as she used to see it in her young days; she followed him out to the mountain-side, where he blew the March on his herd-boy's horn, she drove to church by his side—all his brightness and cleverness lived again for her!

But in Mildrid's soul a new feeling began to stir. Whilst she sat and sang for grandmother, she asked herself: "Will it ever be played for me?" The thought grew upon her, the March spoke to her of such radiant happiness. She saw a bride's crown glittering in its sunshine, and a long, bright future beyond that. Sixteen—and she asked herself: "Shall I, shall I ever have some one sitting beside me, with the Bridal March shining in his eyes? Only think, if father and mother were one day to drive with me in such a procession, with the people greeting us on every side, on to the house where mother was jeered at that day, past Ole Haugen's flower-covered grave, up to the altar, in a glory of happiness! Think what it would be if I could give father and mother that consolation!" And the child's heart swelled, imagining all this to herself, swelled with pride and with devotion to those dear parents who had suffered so much.

These were the first thoughts that she did not confide to Beret. Soon there were more. Beret, who was now eleven, noticed that she was left more to herself, but did not understand that she was being gradually shut out from Mildrid's confidence, till she saw another taken into her place. This was Inga, from the neighbouring farm, a girl of eighteen, their own cousin, newly betrothed. When Mildrid and Inga walked about in the fields, whispering and laughing, with their arms round each other, as girls love to go, poor Beret would throw herself down and cry with jealousy.

The time came on for Mildrid to be confirmed; she made acquaintance with other young people of her own age, and some of them began to come up to Tingvold on Sundays. Mildrid saw them either out of doors or in her grandmother's room. Tingvold had always been a forbidden, and consequently mysteriously attractive place to the young people. But even now, only those with a certain quietness and seriousness of disposition went there, for it could not be denied that there was something subdued about Mildrid, that did not attract every one.

At this particular time there was a great deal of music and singing among the youth of the district. For some reason or other there are such periods, and these periods have their leaders. One of the leaders now was, curiously enough, again of the race of Haugen.

Amongst a people where once on a time, even though it were hundreds of years ago, almost every man and woman sought and found expression for their intensest feelings and experiences in song, and were able themselves to make the verses that gave them relief—amongst such a people the art can never quite die out. Here and there, even though it does not make itself heard, it must exist, ready on occasion to be awakened to new life. But in this district songs had been made and sung from time immemorial. It was by no mere chance that Ole Haugen was born here, and here became what he was. Now it was his grandson in whom the gift had reappeared.

Ole's son had been so much younger than the daughter who had married into the Tingvold family, that the latter, already a married woman, had stood godmother to her little brother. After a life full of changes, this son, as an old man, had come into possession of his father's home and little bit of land far up on the mountain-side; and, strangely enough, not till then did he marry. He had several children, among them a boy called Hans, who seemed to have inherited his grandfather's gifts—not exactly in the way of fiddle-playing, though he did play—but he sang the old songs beautifully and made new ones himself. People's appreciation of his songs was not a little added to by the fact that so few knew himself; there were not many that had even seen him. His old father had been a hunter, and while the boys were quite small, the old man took them out to the hillside and taught them to load and aim a gun. They always remembered how pleased he was when they were able to earn enough with their shooting to pay for their own powder and shot. He did not live long after this, and soon after his death their mother died too, and the children were left to take care of themselves, which they managed to do. The boys hunted and the girls looked after the little hill farm. People turned to look at them when they once in a way showed themselves in the valley; they were so seldom there. It was a long, bad road down. In winter they occasionally came to sell or send off the produce of their hunting; in summer they were busy with the strangers. Their little holding was the highest lying in the district, and it became famed for having that pure mountain air which cures people suffering from their lungs or nerves, better than any yet discovered medicine; every year they had as many summer visitors, from town, and even from abroad, as they could accommodate. They added several rooms to their house, and still it was always full. So these brothers and sisters, from being poor, very poor, came to be quite well-to-do. Intercourse with so many strangers had made them a little different from the other country people—they even knew something of foreign languages. Hans was now twenty-seven. Some years before he had bought up his brothers' and sisters' shares, so that the whole place belonged to him.

Not one of the family had ever set foot in the house of their relations at Tingvold. Endrid and Randi Tingvold, though they had doubtless never put the feeling into words, could just as little bear to hear the name of Haugen as to hear the Bridal March. These children's poor father had been made to feel this, and in consequence, Hans had forbidden his brothers and sisters ever to go to the house. But the girls at Tingvold, who loved music, longed to make acquaintance with Hans, and when they and their girl friends were together, they talked more about the family at Haugen than about anything else. Hans's songs and tunes were sung and danced to, and they were for ever planning how they could manage to meet the young farmer of Haugen.

After this happy time of young companionship came Mildrid's confirmation. Just before it there was a quiet pause, and after it came another. Mildrid, now about seventeen, spent the autumn almost alone with her parents. In spring, or rather summer, she was, like all the other girls after their confirmation, to go to the sœter in charge of cattle. She was delighted at the thought of this, especially as her friend Inga was to be at the next sœter.

At last her longing for the time to come grew so strong that she had no peace at home, and Beret, who was to accompany her, grew restless too. When they got settled in the sœter Beret was quite absorbed in the new, strange life, but Mildrid was still restless. She had her busy times with the cattle and the milk, but there were long idle hours that she did not know how to dispose of. Some days she spent them with Inga, listening to her stories of her lover, but often she had no inclination to go there. She was glad when Inga came to her, and affectionate, as if she wanted to make up for her faithlessness. She seldom talked to Beret, and often when Beret talked to her, answered nothing but Yes or No. When Inga came, Beret took herself off, and when Mildrid went to see Inga, Beret went crying away after the cows, and had the herd-boys for company. Mildrid felt that there was something wrong in all this, but with the best will she could not set it right.

She was sitting one day near the sœter, herding the goats and sheep, because one of the herd-boys had played truant and she had to do his work. It was a warm midday; she was sitting in the shade of a hillock overgrown with birch and underwood; she had thrown off her jacket and taken her knitting in her hand, and was expecting Inga. Something rustled behind her. "There she comes," thought Mildrid, and looked up.

But there was more noise than Inga was likely to make, and such a breaking and cracking among the bushes. Mildrid turned pale, got up, and saw something hairy and a pair of eyes below it—it must be a bear's head! She wanted to scream, but no voice would come; she wanted to run, but could not stir. The thing raised itself up—it was a tall, broad-shouldered man with a fur cap, a gun in his hand. He stopped short among the bushes and looked at her sharply for a second or two, then took a step forward, a jump, and stood in the field beside her. Something moved at her feet, and she gave a little cry; it was his dog, that she had not seen before.

"Oh, dear!" she said; "I thought it was a bear breaking through the bushes, and I got such a fright!" And she tried to laugh.

"Well, it might almost have been that," said he, speaking in a very quiet voice; "Kvas and I were on the track of a bear; but now we have lost it; and if I have a 'Vardöger,'[1] it is certainly a bear."

He smiled. She looked at him. Who can he be? Tall, broad-shouldered, wiry; his eyes restless, so that she could not see them rightly; besides, she was standing quite close to him, just where he had suddenly appeared before her with his dog and his gun.

She felt the inclination to say, "Go away!" but instead she drew back a few steps, and asked: "Who are you?" She was really frightened.

"Hans Haugen," answered the man rather absently; for he was paying attention to the dog, which seemed to have found the track of the bear again. He was just going to add, "Good-bye!" but when he looked at her she was blushing; cheeks, neck, and bosom crimson.

14

"What's the matter?" said he, astonished.

She did not know what to do or where to go, whether to run away or to sit down.

"Who are you?" asked Hans in his turn.

Once again she turned crimson, for to tell him her name was to tell him everything.

"Who are you?" he repeated, as if it were the most natural question in the world, and deserved an answer.

And she could not refuse the answer, though she felt ashamed of herself, and ashamed of her parents, who had neglected their own kindred. The name had to be said. "Mildrid Tingvold," she whispered, and burst into tears.

It was true enough; the Tingvold people had given him little reason to care for them. Of his own free will he would scarcely have spoken to one of them. But he had never foreseen anything like this, and he looked at the girl in amazement. He seemed to remember some story of her mother having cried like that in church on her wedding-day. "Perhaps it's in the family," he thought, and turned to go. "Forgive me for having frightened you," he said, and took his way up the hillside after his dog.

By the time she ventured to look up he had just reached the top of the ridge, and there he turned to look at her. It was only for an instant, for at that moment the dog barked on the other side. Hans gave a start, held his gun in readiness, and hurried on. Mildrid was still gazing at the place where he had stood, when a shot startled her. Could that be the bear? Could it have been so near her?

Off she went, climbing where he had just climbed, till she stood where he had stood, shading her eyes with her hand, and—sure enough, there he was, half hidden by a bush, on his knees beside a huge bear! Before she knew what she was doing, she was down beside him. He gave her a smile of welcome, and explained to her, in his low voice, how it had happened that they had lost the track and the dog had not scented the animal till they were almost upon it. By this time she had forgotten her tears and her bashfulness, and he had drawn his knife to skin the bear on the spot. The flesh was of no value at this time; he meant to bury the carcass and take only the skin. So she held, and he skinned; then she ran down to the sœter for an axe and a spade; and although she still felt afraid of the bear, and it had a bad smell, she kept on helping him till all was finished. By this time it was long past twelve o'clock, and he invited himself to dinner at the sœter. He washed himself and the skin, no small piece of work, and then came in and sat beside her while she finished preparing the food.

He chatted about one thing and another, easily and pleasantly, in the low voice that seems to become natural to people who are much alone. Mildrid gave the shortest answers possible, and when it came to sitting opposite him at the table, she could neither speak nor eat, and there was often silence between them. When she had finished he turned round his chair and filled and lit his pipe. He too was quieter now, and presently he got up. "I must be going," he said, holding out his hand, "it's a long way home from here." Then added, in a still lower voice: "Do you sit every day where you were to-day?" He held her hand for a moment, expecting an answer; but she dared not look up, much less speak. Then she felt him press her hand quickly. "Good-bye, then, and thank you!" he said in a louder tone, and before she could collect herself, she saw him, with the bearskin over his shoulder, the gun in his hand, and the dog at his side, striding away over the heather. There was a dip in the hills just there, and she saw him clear against the sky; his light, firm step taking him quickly away. She watched till he was out of sight, then came outside and sat down, still looking in the same direction.

Not till now was she aware that her heart was beating so violently that she had to press her hands over it. In a minute or two she lay down on the grass, leaning her head on her arm, and began to go carefully over every event of the day. She saw him start up among the bushes and stand before her, strong and active, looking restlessly round. She felt over again the bewilderment and the fright, and her tears of shame. She saw him against the sun, on the height; she heard the shot, and was again on her knees before him, helping him with the skinning of the bear. She heard once more every word that he said, in that low voice that sounded so friendly, and that touched her heart as she thought of it; she listened to it as he sat beside the hearth while she was cooking, and then at table with her. She felt that she had no longer dared to look into his face, so that at last she had made him feel awkward too; for he had grown silent. Then she heard him speak once again, as he took her hand; and she felt his clasp—felt it still, through her whole body. She saw him go away over the heather—away, away!

Would he ever come back? Impossible, after the way she had behaved. How strong, and brave, and self-reliant was everything she had seen of him, and how stupid and miserable all that he had seen of her, from her first scream of fright when the dog touched her, to her blush of shame and her tears; from the clumsy help she gave him, to her slowness in preparing the food. And to think that when he looked at her she was not able to speak; not even to say No, when he asked her if she sat under the hill every day—for she didn't sit there every day! Might not her silence then have seemed like an invitation to him to

16

come and see? Might not her whole miserable helplessness have been misunderstood in the same way? What shame she felt now! She was hot all over with it, and she buried her burning face deeper and deeper in the grass. Then she called up the whole picture once more; all his excellences and her shortcomings; and again the shame of it all overwhelmed her.

She was still lying there when the sound of the bells told her that the cattle were coming home; then she jumped up and began to work. Beret saw as soon as she came that something had happened. Mildrid asked such stupid questions and gave such absurd answers, and altogether behaved in such an extraordinary way, that she several times just stopped and stared at her. When it came to supper-time, and Mildrid, instead of taking her place at the table, went and sat down outside, saying that she had just had dinner, Beret was as intensely on the alert as a dog who scents game at hand. She took her supper and went to bed. The sisters slept in the same bed, and, as Mildrid did not come, Beret got up softly once or twice to look if her sister were still sitting out there, and if she were alone. Yes, she was there, and alone.

Eleven o'clock, and then twelve, and then one, and still Mildrid sat and Beret waked. She pretended to be asleep when Mildrid came at last, and Mildrid moved softly, so softly; but her sister heard her sobbing, and when she had got into bed she heard her say her usual evening prayer so sadly, heard her whisper: "O God, help me, help me!" It made Beret so unhappy that she could not get to sleep even now. She felt her sister restlessly changing from one position to another; she saw her at last giving it up, throwing aside the covering, and lying open-eyed, with her hands below her head, staring into vacancy. She saw and heard no more, for at last she fell asleep.

When she awoke next morning Mildrid's place was empty. Beret jumped up; the sun was high in the sky; the cattle were away long ago. She found her breakfast set ready, took it hurriedly, and went out and saw Mildrid at work, but looking ill. Beret said that she was going to hurry after the cattle. Mildrid said nothing in answer, but gave her a glance as though of thanks. The younger girl stood a minute thinking, and then went off.

Mildrid looked round; yes, she was alone. She hastily put away the dishes, leaving everything else as it was. Then she washed herself and changed her dress, took her knitting, and set off up the hill.

She had not the new strength of the new day, for she had hardly slept or eaten anything for twenty-four hours. She walked in a dream, and knew nothing clearly till she was at the place where she had sat yesterday.

Hardly had she seated herself when she thought: "If he were to come and find me here, he would believe—" She started up mechanically. There was his dog on the hillside. It stood still and looked at her, then rushed down to her, wagging its tail. Her heart stopped beating. There—there he stood, with his gun gleaming in the sun, just as he had stood yesterday. To-day he had come another way. He smiled to her, ran down, and stood before her. She had given a little scream and sunk down on the grass again. It was more than she could do to stand up; she let her knitting drop, and put her hands up to her face. He did not say a word. He lay down on the grass in front of her, and looked up at her, the dog at his side with its eyes fixed on him. She felt that though she was turning her head away, he could see her hot blush, her eyes, her whole face. She heard him breathing quickly; she thought she felt his breath on her hand. She did not want him to speak, and yet his silence was dreadful. She knew that he must understand why she was sitting there; and greater shame than this no one had ever felt. But it was not right of him, either, to have come, and still worse of him to be lying there.

Then she felt him take one of her hands and hold it tight, then the other, so that she had to turn a little that way; he drew her gently, but strongly and firmly towards him with eye and hand, till she was at his side, her head fallen on his shoulder. She felt him stroke her hair with one hand, but she dared not look up. Presently she broke into passionate weeping at the thought of her shameful behaviour.

"Yes, you may cry," said he, "but I will laugh; what has happened to us two is matter both for laughter and for tears."

His voice shook. And now he bent over her and whispered that the farther away he went from her yesterday the nearer he seemed to be to her. The feeling overmastered him so, that when he reached his little shooting cabin, where he had a German officer with him this summer, recruiting after the war, he left the guest to take care of himself, and wandered farther up the mountain. He spent the night on the heights, sometimes sitting, sometimes wandering about. He went home to breakfast, but away again immediately. He was twenty-eight now, no longer a boy, and he felt that either this girl must be his or it would go badly with him. He wandered to the place where they had met yesterday; he did not expect that she would be there again; but when he saw her, he felt that he must make the venture; and when he came to see that she was feeling just as he was—"Why, then"—and he raised her head gently. And she had stopped crying, and his eyes shone so that she had to look into them, and then she turned red and put her head down again.

He went on talking in his low, half-whispering voice. The sun shone through the tree-tops, the birches trembled in the breeze, the birds mingled their song with the sound of a little stream rippling over its stony bed.

How long the two sat there together, neither of them knew. At last the dog startled them. He had made several excursions, and each time had come back and lain down beside them again; but now he ran barking down the hill. They both jumped up and stood for a minute listening. But nothing appeared. Then they looked at each other again, and Hans lifted her up in his arms. She had not been lifted like this since she was a child, and there was something about it that made her feel helpless. When he looked up beaming into her face, she bent and put her arms round his neck—he was now her strength, her future, her happiness, her life itself—she resisted no longer.

Nothing was said. He held her tight; she clung to him. He carried her to the place where she had sat at first, and sat down there with her on his knee. She did not unloose her arms, she only bent her head close down to his so as to hide her face from him. He was just going to force her to let him look into it, when some one right in front of them called in a voice of astonishment: "Mildrid!"

It was Inga, who had come up after the dog. Mildrid sprang to her feet, looked at her friend for an instant, then went up to her, put one arm round her neck, and laid her head on her shoulder. Inga put her arm round Mildrid's waist. "Who is he?" she whispered, and Mildrid felt her tremble, but said nothing. Inga knew who he was—knew him quite well—but could not believe her own eyes. Then Hans came slowly forward, "I thought you knew me," he said quietly; "I am Hans Haugen." When she heard his voice, Mildrid lifted her head. How good and true he looked as he stood there! He held out his hand; she went forward and took it, and looked at her friend with a flush of mingled shame and joy.

Then Hans took his gun and said good-bye, whispering to Mildrid: "You may be sure I'll come soon again!"

The girls walked with him as far as the sœter, and watched him, as Mildrid had done yesterday, striding away over the heather in the sunlight. They stood as long as they could see him; Mildrid, who was leaning on Inga, would not let her go; Inga felt that she did not want her to move or speak. From time to time one or the other whispered: "He's looking back!" When he was out of sight Mildrid turned round to Inga and said: "Don't ask me anything. I can't tell you about it!" She held her tight for a second, and then they walked towards the sœter-house. Mildrid remembered now how she had left all her work undone. Inga helped her with it. They spoke very little, and only about the work. Just once Mildrid stopped, and whispered: "Isn't he handsome?"

She set out some dinner, but could eat little herself, though she felt the need both of food and sleep. Inga left as soon as she could, for she saw that Mildrid would rather be alone. Then Mildrid lay down on her bed. She was lying, half asleep already, thinking over the events of the morning, and trying to remember the nicest things that Hans had said, when it suddenly occurred to her to ask herself what she had answered. Then it flashed upon her that during their whole meeting she had not spoken, not said a single word!

She sat up in bed and said to herself: "He could not have gone far till this must have struck him too—and what can he have thought? He must take me for a creature without a will, going about in a dream. How can he go on caring for me? Yesterday it was not till he had gone away from me that he found out he cared for me at all—what will he find out to-day?" she asked herself with a shiver of dread. She got up, went out, and sat down where she had sat so long yesterday.

All her life Mildrid had been accustomed to take herself to account for her behaviour; circumstances had obliged her to walk carefully. Now, thinking over what had happened these last two days, it struck her forcibly that she had behaved without tact, without thought, almost without modesty. She had never read or heard about anything happening like this; she looked at it from the peasant's point of view, and none take these matters more strictly than they. It is seemly to control one's feelings—it is honourable to be slow to show them. She, who had done this all her life, and consequently been respected by every one, had in one day given herself to a man she had never seen before! Why, he himself must be the first to despise her! It showed how bad things were, that she dared not tell what had happened, not even to Inga!

With the first sound of the cow-bells in the distance came Beret, to find her sister sitting on the bench in front of the sœter-house, looking half dead. Beret stood in front of her till she was forced to raise her head and look at her. Mildrid's eyes were red with crying, and her whole expression was one of suffering. But it changed to surprise when she saw Beret's face, which was scarlet with excitement.

"Whatever is the matter with you?" she exclaimed.

"Nothing!" answered Beret, standing staring fixedly at Mildrid, who at last looked away, and got up to go and attend to the cows.

The sisters did not meet again till supper, when they sat opposite to each other. Mildrid was not able to eat more then a few mouthfuls. She sat and looked absently at the others, oftenest at Beret, who ate on steadily, gulping down her food like a hungry dog.

"Have you had nothing to eat to-day?" asked Mildrid.

"No!" answered Beret, and ate on. Presently Mildrid spoke again: "Have you not been with the herds then?"

"No!" answered her sister and both of the boys. Before them Mildrid would not ask more, and afterwards her own morbid reflections took possession of her again, and along with them the feeling that she was no fit person to be in charge of Beret. This was one more added to the reproaches she made to herself all that long summer evening and far into the night.

There she sat, on the bench by the door, till the blood-red clouds changed gradually to cold grey, no peace and no desire for sleep coming to her. The poor child had never before been in real distress. Oh, how she prayed! She stopped and she began again; she repeated prayers that she had learned, and she made up petitions of her own. At last, utterly exhausted, she went to bed.

There she tried once more to collect her thoughts for a final struggle with the terrible question, Should she give him up or not? But she had no strength left; she could only say over and over again: "Help me, O God! help me!" She went on like this for a long time, sometimes saying it in to herself, sometimes out loud. All at once she got such a fright that she gave a loud scream. Beret was kneeling up in bed looking at her; her sparkling eyes, hot face, and short breathing showing a terrible state of excitement.

"Who is he?" she whispered, almost threateningly. Mildrid, crushed by her self-torture, and worn out in soul and body, could not answer; she began to cry.

"Who is he?" repeated the other, closer to her face; "you needn't try to hide it any longer; I was watching you to-day the whole time!"

Mildrid held up her arms as if to defend herself, but Beret beat them back, looked straight into her eyes, and again repeated, "Who is he, I say?"

"Beret, Beret!" moaned Mildrid; "have I ever been anything but kind to you since you were a little child. Why are you so cruel to me now that I am in trouble?"

Then Beret, moved by her tears, let go her arms; but her short hard breathing still betrayed her excitement. "Is it Hans Haugen?" she whispered.

There was a moment of breathless suspense, and then Mildrid whispered back: "Yes"—and began to cry again.

Beret drew down her arms once more; she wanted to see her face. "Why did you not tell me about it, Mildrid?" she asked, with the same fierce eagerness.

"Beret, I didn't know it myself. I never saw him till yesterday. And as soon as I saw him I loved him, and let him see it, and that is what is making me so unhappy, so unhappy that I feel as if I must die of it!"

"You never saw him before yesterday?" screamed Beret, so astonished that she could hardly believe it.

21

"Never in my life!" replied Mildrid. "Isn't it shameful, Beret?"

But Beret threw her arms round her sister's neck, and kissed her over and over again.

"Dear, sweet Mildrid, I'm so glad!" she whispered, now radiant with joy. "I'm so glad, so glad!" and she kissed her once more. "And you'll see how I can keep a secret, Mildrid!" She hugged her to her breast, but sat up again, and said sorrowfully: "And you thought I couldn't do it; O Mildrid! not even when it was about you!"

And now it was Beret's turn to cry. "Why have you put me away? Why have you taken Inga instead of me? You've made me so dreadfully unhappy, Mildrid! O Mildrid, you don't know how I love you!" and she clung to her. Then Mildrid kissed her, and told her that she had done it without thinking what she was doing, but that now she would never again put her aside, and would tell her everything, because she was so good and true and faithful.

The sisters lay for a little with their arms round each other; then Beret sat up again; she wanted to look into her sister's face in the light of the summer night, that was gradually taking a tinge of red from the coming dawn. Then she burst out with: "Mildrid, how handsome he is! How did he come? How did you see him first? What did he say? Do tell me about it!"

And Mildrid now poured out to her sister all that a few hours ago it had seemed to her she could never tell to anybody. She was sometimes interrupted by Beret's throwing her arms round her and hugging her, but she went on again with all the more pleasure. It seemed to her like a strange legend of the woods. They laughed and they cried. Sleep had gone from them both. The sun found them still entranced by this wonderful tale—Mildrid lying down or resting on one elbow and talking, Beret kneeling beside her, her mouth half open, her eyes sparkling, from time to time giving a little cry of delight.

They got up together and did their work together, and when they had finished, and for the sake of appearances taken a little breakfast, they prepared for the meeting with Hans. He was sure to come soon! They dressed themselves out in their best, and went up to Mildrid's place on the hill. Beret showed where she had lain hidden yesterday. The dog had found her out, she said, and paid her several visits. The weather was fine to-day too, though there were some clouds in the sky. The girls found plenty to say to each other, till it was about the time when Hans might be expected. Beret ran once or twice up to the top of the hill, to see if he were in sight, but there was no sign of him. Then they began to grow impatient, and at last Mildrid got so excited that Beret was frightened. She tried to soothe her by reminding her that Hans was not his own master; that he had left the German gentleman two whole days to fish and shoot alone, and prepare food for himself; and that he would hardly dare to leave him a third. And Mildrid acknowledged that this might be so.

"What do you think father and mother will say to all this?" asked Beret, just to divert Mildrid's thoughts. She repented the moment the words were uttered. Mildrid turned pale and stared at Beret, who stared back at her. Beret wondered if her sister had never thought of this till now, and said so. Yes; she had thought of it, but as of something very far off. The fear of what Hans Haugen might think of her, the shame of her own weakness and stupidity, had so occupied her mind that they had left no room for anything else. But now things suddenly changed round, and she could think of nothing but her parents.

Beret again tried to comfort her. Whenever father and mother saw Hans, they would feel that Mildrid was right—they would never make her unhappy who had given them their greatest happiness. Grandmother would help her. No one could say a word against Hans Haugen, and *he* would never give her up! Mildrid heard all this, but did not take it in, for she was thinking of something else, and to get time to think it out rightly, she asked Beret to go and prepare the dinner. And Beret walked slowly away, looking back several times.

Mildrid wanted to be left alone a little to make up her mind whether she should go at once and tell her parents. It seemed a terrible matter to her in her excited, exhausted state. She felt now that it would be a sin if she saw Hans again without their knowledge. She had done very wrong in engaging herself to him without having their consent; but she had been in a manner surprised into that; it had come about almost without her will. Her duty now, though, was clearly to go and tell them.

She rose to her feet, with a new light in her eyes. She would do what was right. Before Hans stood there again, her parents should know all. "That's it!" she said, aloud, as if some one were there, and then hurried down to the sœter to tell Beret. But Beret was nowhere to be seen. "Beret! Beret!" shouted Mildrid, but only the echoes gave answer. Excited Mildrid was already, but now she got frightened too. Beret's great eyes, as she asked: "What do you think father and mother will say to this?" seemed to grow ever greater and more threatening. Surely *she* could never have gone off to tell them? Yet it would be just like her hasty way to think she would settle the thing at once, and bring comfort to her sister. To be sure that was it! And if Beret reached home before her, father and mother would get a wrong idea of everything!

Off Mildrid went, down the road that led to the valley. She walked unconsciously faster and faster, carried away by ever-increasing excitement; till her head began to turn and her breathing to get oppressed. She had to sit down for a rest. Sitting did not seem to help her, so she stretched herself out,

23

resting her head on her arm, and lay there, feeling forsaken, helpless, almost betrayed—by affection it was true—but still betrayed.

In a few moments she was asleep! For two days and nights she had hardly slept or eaten; and she had no idea of the effect this had had on her mind and body—the child who till now had eaten and slept so regularly and peacefully in her quiet home. How was it possible that she could understand anything at all of what had happened to her? All that she had been able to give to her affectionate but melancholy parents out of her heart's rich store of love, was a kind of watchful care; in her grandmother's brighter home longings for something more had often come over her, but there was nothing even there to satisfy them. So now when love's full spring burst upon her, she stood amidst its rain of blossoms frightened and ashamed.

Tormented by her innocent conscience, the poor tired child had run a race with herself till she fell—now she slept, caressed by the pure mountain breeze.

Beret had not gone home, but away to fetch Hans Haugen. She had far to go, and most of the way was unknown to her. It went first by the edge of a wood, and then higher over bare flats, not quite safe from wild animals, which she knew had been seen there lately. But she went on, for Hans really must come. If he did not, she was sure things would go badly with Mildrid; she seemed so changed to-day.

In spite of her anxiety about Mildrid, Beret's heart was light, and she stepped merrily on, her thoughts running all the time on this wonderful adventure. She could think of no one better or grander than Hans Haugen, and none but the very best was good enough for Mildrid. There was nothing whatever to be surprised at in Mildrid's giving herself up to him at once; just as little as in his at once falling in love with her. If father and mother could not be brought to understand this, they must just be left to do as they chose, and the two must fight their own battle as her great-grandparents had done, and her grandparents too—and she began to sing the old Bridal March. Its joyful tones sounded far over the bare heights and seemed to die away among the clouds.

When she got right on the top of the hill she was crossing, she stood and shouted "Hurrah!" From here she could see only the last strip of cultivated land on the farther side of their valley; and on this side the upper margin of the forest, above it stretches of heather, and where she stood, nothing but boulders and flat rocks. She flew from stone to stone in the light air. She knew that Hans's hut lay in the direction of the snow mountain whose top stood out above all the others, and presently she thought that she must be getting near it. To get a better look around she climbed up on to an enormous stone, and from

24

the top of it she saw a mountain lake just below. Whether it was a rock or a hut she saw by the water's edge she could not be sure; one minute it looked like a hut, the next like a big stone. But she knew that his cabin lay by a mountain lake. Yes, that must be it, for there came a boat rowing round the point. Two men were in the boat—they must be Hans and the German officer. Down she jumped and off again. But what had looked so near was really far off, and she ran and ran, excited by the thought of meeting Hans Haugen.

Hans sat quietly in his boat with the German, ignorant of all the disturbance he had caused. *He* had never known what it was to be frightened; nor had he ever till now known the feeling of being in love. As soon as he did feel it, it was intolerable to him until he had settled the matter. Now it was settled, and he was sitting there setting words to the Bridal March!

He was not much of a poet, but he made out something about their ride to church, and the refrain of every verse told of their meeting in the wood. He whistled and fished and felt very happy; and the German fished away quietly and left him in peace.

A halloo sounded from the shore, and both he and the bearded German looked up and saw a girl waving. They exchanged a few words and rowed ashore. Hans jumped out and tied up the boat, and they lifted out the guns, coats, fish, and fishing tackle; the German went away towards the cabin, but Hans with his load came up to Beret, who was standing on a stone a little way off.

"Who are you?" he asked gently.

"Beret, Mildrid's sister," she answered, blushing, and he blushed too. But the next moment he turned pale.

"Is there anything the matter?"

"No! just that you must come. She can't bear to be left alone just now."

He stood a minute and looked at her, then turned and went towards the hut. The German was standing outside, hanging up his fishing tackle; Hans hung up his, and they spoke together, and then went in. Ever since Beret's halloo, two dogs, shut up in the cabin, had been barking with all their might. When the men opened the door they burst out, but were at once sternly called back. It was some time before Hans came out again. He had changed his clothes, and had his gun and dog with him. The German gentleman came to the door, and they shook hands as if saying good-bye for a considerable time. Hans came up quickly to Beret.

"Can you walk fast?" he asked.

"Of course I can."

And off they went, she running, the dog far ahead.

Beret's message had entirely changed the current of Hans's thoughts. It had never occurred to him before that Mildrid might not have the same happy, sure feeling about their engagement that he had. But now he saw how natural it was that she should be uneasy about her parents; and how natural, too, that she should feel alarmed by the hurried rush in which everything had come about. He understood it so well now that he was perfectly astonished at himself for not having thought of it before—and on he strode.

Even on him the suddenness of the meeting with Mildrid, and the violence of their feelings, had at first made a strange impression; what must she, a child, knowing nothing but the quiet reserve of her parents' house, have felt, thus launched suddenly on the stormy sea of passion!—and on he strode.

While he was marching along, lost in these reflections, Beret was trotting at his side, always, when she could, with her face turned towards his. Now and then he had caught a glimpse of her big eyes and flaming cheeks; but his thoughts were like a veil over his sight; he saw her indistinctly, and then suddenly not at all. He turned round; she was a good way behind, toiling after him as hard as she could. She had been too proud to say that she could not keep up with him any longer. He stood and waited till she made up to him, breathless, with tears in her eyes. "Ah! I'm walking too fast," and he held out his hand. She was panting so that she could not answer. "Let us sit down a little," he said, drawing her to him; "come!" and he made her sit close to him. If possible she got redder than before, and did not look at him; and she drew breath so painfully that it seemed as if she were almost choking. "I'm so thirsty!" was the first thing she managed to say. They rose and he looked round, but there was no stream near. "We must wait till we get a little farther on," he said; "and anyhow it wouldn't be good for you to drink just now."

So they sat down again, she on a stone in front of him.

"I ran the whole way," she said, as if to excuse herself—and presently added, "and I have had no dinner," and after another pause—"and I didn't sleep last night."

Instead of expressing any sympathy with her, he asked sharply: "Then I suppose Mildrid did not sleep last night either? And she has not eaten, I saw that myself, not for"—he thought a little—"not for ever so long."

He rose. "Can you go on now?"

"I think so."

He took her hand, and they set off again at a tremendous pace. Soon he saw that she could not keep it up, so he took off his coat, gave it to her to hold, and lifted her up and carried her. She did not want him to do it, but he just went easily off with her, and Beret held on by his neckerchief, for she dared not touch him. Soon she said that she had got her breath and could run quite well again, so he put her down, took his coat and hung it over his gun—and off they went! When they came to a stream they stopped and rested a little before she took a drink. As she got up he gave her a friendly smile, and said: "You're a good little one."

Evening was coming on when they reached the sœter. They looked in vain for Mildrid, both there and at her place on the hillside. Their calls died away in the distance, and when Hans noticed the dog standing snuffing at something they felt quite alarmed. They ran to look—it was her little shawl. At once Hans set the dog to seek the owner of the shawl. He sprang off, and they after him, across the hill and down on the other side, towards Tingvold. Could she have gone home? Beret told of her own thoughtless question and its consequences, and Hans said he saw it all. Beret began to cry.

"Shall we go after her or not?" said Hans.

"Yes, yes!" urged Beret, half distracted. But first they would have to go to the next sœter, and ask their neighbours to send some one to attend to the cows for them. While they were still talking about this, and at the same time following the dog, they saw him stop and look back, wagging his tail. They ran to him, and there lay Mildrid!

She was lying with her head on her arm, her face half buried in the heather. They stepped up gently; the dog licked her hands and cheek, and she stretched herself and changed her position, but slept on. "Let her sleep!" whispered

27

Hans; "and you go and put in the cows. I hear the bells." As Beret was running off he went after her. "Bring some food with you when you come back," he whispered. Then he sat down a little way from Mildrid, made the dog lie down beside him, and sat and held him to keep him from barking.

It was a cloudy evening. The near heights and the mountain-tops were grey; it was very quiet; there was not even a bird to be seen. He sat or lay, with his hand on the dog. He had soon settled what to arrange with Mildrid when she awoke. There was no cloud in their future; he lay quietly looking up into the sky. He knew that their meeting was a miracle. God Himself had told him that they were to go through life together.

He fell to working away at the Bridal March again, and the words that came to him now expressed the quiet happiness of the hour.

It was about eight o'clock when Beret came back, bringing food with her. Mildrid was still sleeping. Beret set down what she was carrying, looked at them both for a minute, and then went and sat down a little way from them. Nearly an hour passed, Beret getting up from time to time to keep herself from falling asleep. Soon after nine Mildrid awoke. She turned several times, at last opened her eyes, saw where she was lying, sat up, and noticed the others. She was still bewildered with sleep, so that she did not take in rightly where she was or what she saw, till Hans rose and came smiling towards her. Then she held out her hands to him.

He sat down beside her:

"You've had a sleep now, Mildrid?"

"Yes, I've slept now."

"And you're hungry?"

"Yes, I'm hungry——" and Beret came forward with the food. She looked at it and then at them. "Have I slept long?" she asked.

"Well, it's almost nine o'clock; look at the sun!"

Not till now did she begin to remember everything.

"Have you sat here long?"

"No, not very long—but you must eat!" She began to do so. "You were on your way down to the valley?" asked Hans gently, with his head nearer hers. She blushed and whispered, "Yes."

"To-morrow, when you've really had a good sleep and rest, we'll go down together."

Her eyes looked into his, first in surprise, then as if she were thanking him, but she said nothing.

After this she seemed to revive; she asked Beret where *she* had been, and Beret told that she had gone to fetch Hans, and he told all the rest. Mildrid ate and listened, and yielded gradually once again to the old fascination. She laughed when Hans told her how the dog had found her, and had licked her face without wakening her. He was at this moment greedily watching every bite she took, and she began to share with him.

As soon as she had finished, they went slowly towards the sœter—and Beret was soon in bed. The two sat on the bench outside the door. Small rain was beginning to fall, but the broad eaves kept them from feeling it. The mist closed round the sœter, and shut them in in a sort of magic circle. It was neither day nor night, but dark rather than light. Each softly spoken word brought more confidence into their talk. Now for the first time they were really speaking to each other. He asked her so humbly to forgive him for not having remembered that she must feel differently from him, and that she had parents who must be consulted. She confessed her fear, and then she told him that he was the first real, strong, self-reliant man she had ever known, and that this, and other things she had heard about him, had—she would not go on.

But in their trembling happiness everything spoke, to the slightest breath they drew. That wonderful intercourse began of soul with soul, which in most cases precedes and prepares for the first embrace, but with these two came after it. The first timid questions came through the darkness, the first timid answers found their way back. The words fell softly, like spirit sounds on the night air. At last Mildrid took courage to ask hesitatingly if her behaviour had not sometimes struck him as very strange. He assured her that he had never thought it so, never once. Had he not noticed that she had not said one word all the time they were together yesterday? No, he had not noticed that. Had he not wondered at her going off down to her parents? No, he had thought it only right of her. Had he not thought (for a long time she would not say this, but at last the words came, in a whisper, with her face turned away), had he not thought that she had let things go too quickly? No, he had only thought how beautifully everything had happened. But what had he thought of the way she had cried at their first meeting? Well, at the time it had puzzled him, but now he understood it, quite well—and he was glad she was like that.

All these answers made her so happy that she felt she wanted to be alone. And as if he had guessed this, he got up quietly and said that now she must go to bed. She rose. He nodded and went off slowly towards the shed where he was to sleep; she hurried in, undressed, and when she had got into bed she folded her hands and thanked God. Oh, how she thanked Him! Thanked Him for Hans's love, and patience, and kindness—she had not words enough!

Thanked Him for all, all, everything—even for the suffering of the last two days—for had it not made the joy all the greater? Thanked Him for their having been alone up there at this time, and prayed Him to be with her to-morrow when she went down to her parents, then turned her thoughts again to Hans, and gave thanks for him once more, oh, how gratefully!

When she came out of the sœter-house in the morning, Beret was still sleeping. Hans was standing in the yard. He had been punishing the dog for rousing a ptarmigan, and it was now lying fawning on him. When he saw Mildrid he let the dog out of disgrace; it jumped up on him and her, barked and caressed them, and was like a living expression of their own bright morning happiness. Hans helped Mildrid and the boys with the morning work. By the time they had done it all and were ready to sit down to breakfast, Beret was up and ready too. Every time Hans looked at her she turned red, and when Mildrid after breakfast stood playing with his watch chain while she spoke to him, Beret hurried out, and was hardly to be found when it was time for the two to go.

"Mildrid," said Hans, coming close to her and walking slowly, when they had got on a little way, "I have been thinking about something that I didn't say to you yesterday." His voice sounded so serious that she looked up into his face. He went on slowly, without looking at her; "I want to ask you if—God granting that we get each other—if you will go home with me after the wedding and live at Haugen."

She turned red, and presently answered evasively:

"What will father and mother say to that?"

He walked on without answering for a minute, and then said:

"I did not think that mattered so much, if we two were agreed about it."

This was the first time he had said a thing that hurt her. She made no reply. He seemed to be waiting for one, and when none came, added gently:

"I wanted us two to be alone together, to get accustomed to each other."

Now she began to understand him better, but she could not answer. He walked on as before, not looking at her, and now quite silent. She felt uneasy, stole a glance at him, and saw that he had turned quite pale.

"Hans!" she cried, and stood still without being conscious of doing it. Hans stopped too, looked quickly at her, and then down at his gun, which he was resting on the ground and turning in his hand.

"Can you not go with me to my home?" His voice was very low, but all at once he looked her straight in the face.

"Yes, I can!" she answered quickly. Her eyes looked calmly into his, but a faint blush came over her cheeks. He changed his gun into his left hand, and held out the right to her.

"Thank you!" he whispered, holding hers in a firm clasp; Then they went on.

She was brooding over one thought all the time, and at last could not keep it in: "You don't know my father and mother."

He went on a little before he answered: "No, but when you come and live at Haugen, I'll have time then to get to know them."

"They are so good!" added Mildrid.

"So I have heard from every one." He said this decidedly, but coldly.

Before she had time to think or say anything more, he began to tell about *his* home, his brothers and sisters, and their industry, affectionateness, and cheerfulness; about the poverty they had raised themselves from; about the tourists who came and all the work they gave; about the house, and especially about the new one he would now build for her and himself. She was to be the mistress of the whole place—but they would help her in everything; they would all try to make her life happy, he not least. As he talked they walked on faster; he spoke warmly, came closer to her, and at last they walked hand in hand.

It could not be denied that his love for his home and his family made a strong impression on her, and there was a great attraction in the newness of it all; but behind this feeling lay one of wrong-doing towards her parents, her dear, kind parents. So she began again: "Hans! mother is getting old now, and father is older; they have had a great deal of trouble—they need help; they've worked so hard, and—" she either would not or could not say more.

He walked slower and looked at her, smiling. "Mildrid, you mean that they have settled to give you the farm?"

She blushed, but did not answer.

"Well, then—we'll let that alone till the time comes. When they want us to take their places, it's for them to ask us to do it." He said this very gently and tenderly, but she felt what it meant. Thoughtful of others, as she always was, and accustomed to consider their feelings before her own, she yielded in this too. But very soon they came to where they could see Tingvold in the valley below them. She looked down at it, and then at him, as if it could speak for itself.

The big sunny fields on the hill slope, with the wood encircling and sheltering them, the house and farm buildings a little in the shadow, but big and fine—it all looked so beautiful. The valley, with its rushing, winding river, stretched away down beyond, with farm after farm in the bottom and on its slopes on both sides—but none, not one to equal Tingvold—none so fertile or so pleasant to the eye, none so snugly sheltered, and yet commanding the whole valley. When she saw that Hans was struck by the sight, she reddened with joy.

"Yes," he said, in answer to her unspoken question—"yes, it is true; Tingvold is a fine place; it would be hard to find its equal."

He smiled and bent down to her. "But I care more for you, Mildrid, than for Tingvold; and perhaps—you care more for me than for Tingvold?"

When he took it this way she could say no more. He looked so happy too; he sat down, and she beside him.

"Now I'm going to sing something for you," he whispered.

She felt glad. "I've never heard you sing," she said.

"No, I know you have not; and though people talk about my singing, you must not think it's anything very great. There's only this about it, that it comes upon me sometimes, and then I *must* sing."

He sat thinking for a good while, and then he sang her the song that he had made for their own wedding to the tune of her race's Bridal March. Quite softly he sang it, but with such exultation as she had never heard in any voice before. She looked down on her home, the house she was to drive away from on that day; followed the road with her eyes down to the bridge across the river, and along on the other side right up to the church, which lay on a height, among birch-trees, with a group of houses near it. It was not a very clear day, but the subdued light over the landscape was in sympathy with the subdued picture in her mind. How many hundred times had she not driven that road in fancy, only she never knew with whom! The words and the tune entranced her; the peculiar warm, soft voice seemed to touch the very depths of her being; her eyes were full, but she was not crying; nor was she laughing. She was sitting with her hand on his, now looking at him, now over the valley, when she saw smoke beginning to rise from the chimney of her home; the fire was being lit for making the dinner. This was an omen; she turned to Hans and pointed. He had finished his song now, and they sat still and looked.

Very soon they were on their way down through the birch wood, and Hans was having trouble with the dog, to make him keep quiet. Mildrid's heart began to throb. Hans arranged with her that he would stay behind, but near the house; it was better that she should go in first alone. He carried her over one or two marshy places, and he felt that her hands were cold. "Don't think of what you're to say," he whispered; "just wait and see how things come." She gave no sound in answer, nor did she look at him.

They came out of the wood—the last part had been big dark fir-trees, among which they had walked slowly, he quietly telling her about her great-grandfather's wooing of his father's sister, Aslaug; an old, strange story, which she only half heard, but which all the same helped her—came out of the wood into the open fields and meadows; and he became quiet too. Now she turned to him, and her look expressed such a great dread of what was before her that it made him feel wretched. He found no words of encouragement; the matter concerned him too nearly. They walked on a little farther, side by side, some bushes between them and the house concealing them from its inhabitants. When they got so near that he thought she must now go on alone, he whistled softly to the dog, and she took this as the sign that they must part. She stopped and looked utterly unhappy and forlorn; he whispered to her: "I'll be praying for you here, Mildrid—and I'll come when you need me." She gave him a kind of distracted look of thanks; she was really unable either to think or to see clearly. Then she walked on.

As soon as she came out from the bushes she saw right into the big room of the main building—right through it—for it had windows at both ends, one looking up towards the wood and one down the valley. Hans had seated himself behind the nearest bush, with the dog at his side, and he too could see everything in the room; at this moment there was no one in it. Mildrid looked back once when she came to the barn, and he nodded to her. Then she went round the end of the barn, into the yard.

Everything stood in its old, accustomed order, and it was very quiet. Some hens were walking on the barn-steps. The wooden framework for the stacks had been brought out and set up against the storehouse wall since she was there last; that was the only change she saw. She turned to the right to go first into grandmother's house, her fear tempting her to take this little respite before meeting her parents; when, just between the two houses, at the wood-block, she came on her father, fitting a handle to an axe. He was in his knitted jersey with the braces over it, bareheaded, his thin long hair blowing in the breeze that was beginning to come up from the valley. He looked well, and almost cheerful at his work, and she took courage at the sight. He did not notice her, she had come so quietly and cautiously over the flagstones.

"Good morning!" she said in a low voice.

He looked at her in surprise for a moment.

"Is that you, Mildrid? Is there anything the matter?" he added hastily, examining her face.

"No," she said, and blushed a little. But he kept his eyes on hers, and she did not dare to look up.

Then he put down the axe, saying:

"Let us go in to mother!"

On the way he asked one or two questions about things up at the sœter, and got satisfactory answers.

"Now Hans sees us going in," thought Mildrid, as they passed a gap between the barn and some of the smaller outhouses.

When they got into the living-room, her father went to the door leading into the kitchen, opened it, and called:

"Come here, mother! Mildrid has come down."

"Why, Mildrid, has anything gone wrong?" was answered from the kitchen.

"No," replied Mildrid from behind her father, and then coming to the door herself, she went into the kitchen and stood beside her mother, who was sitting by the hearth paring potatoes and putting them in the pot.

Her mother now looked as inquiringly at her as her father had done, with the same effect. Then Randi set away the potato dish, went to the outer door and spoke to some one there, came back again, took off her kitchen apron and washed her hands, and they went together into the room.

Mildrid knew her parents, and knew that these preparations meant that they expected something unusual. She had had little courage before, but now it grew less. Her father took his raised seat close to the farthest away window, the one that looked down the valley. Her mother sat on the same bench, but nearer the kitchen. Mildrid seated herself on the opposite one, in front of the table. Hans could see her there; and he could see her father, right in the face, but her mother he could hardly see.

Her mother asked, as her father had done before, about things at the sœter; got the same information and a little more; for she asked more particularly. It was evident that both sides were making this subject last as long as possible, but it was soon exhausted. In the pause that came, both parents looked at Mildrid. She avoided the look, and asked what news there was of the neighbours. This subject was also drawn out as long as possible, but it came to an end too. The same silence, the same expectant eyes turned on the daughter. There was nothing left for her to ask about, and she began to rub her hand back and forwards on the bench.

"Have you been in at grandmother's?" asked her mother, who was beginning to get frightened.

34

No, she had not been there. This meant then that their daughter had something particular to say to *them*, and it could not with any seemliness be put off longer.

"There is something that I must tell you," she got out at last, with changing colour and downcast eyes.

Her father and mother exchanged troubled looks. Mildrid raised her head and looked at them with great imploring eyes.

"What is it, my child?" asked her mother anxiously.

"I am betrothed," said Mildrid; hung her head again, and burst into tears.

No more stunning blow could have fallen on the quiet circle. The parents sat looking at each other, pale and silent. The steady, gentle Mildrid, for whose careful ways and whose obedience they had so often thanked God, had, without asking their advice, without their knowledge, taken life's most important step, a step that was also decisive for *their* past and future. Mildrid felt each thought along with them, and fear stopped her crying.

Her father asked gently and slowly: "To whom, my child?"

After a silence came the whispered answer: "To Hans Haugen."

No name or event connected with Haugen had been mentioned in that room for more than twenty years. In her parents' opinion nothing but evil had come to Tingvold from there. Mildrid again knew their thoughts: she sat motionless, awaiting her sentence.

Her father spoke again mildly and slowly: "We don't know the man, neither I nor your mother—and we didn't know that you knew him."

"And I didn't know him either," said Mildrid.

The astonished parents looked at each other. "How did it happen then?" It was her mother who asked this.

"That is what I don't know myself," said Mildrid.

"But, my child, surely you're mistress of your own actions?"

Mildrid did not answer.

"We thought," added her father gently, "that we could be quite sure of *you*."

Mildrid did not answer.

"But how did it happen?" repeated her mother more impatiently; "you must know that!"

"No, I don't know it—I only know that I could not help it—no, I couldn't!" She was sitting holding on to the bench with both hands.

"God forgive and help you! Whatever came over you?"

Mildrid gave no answer.

Her father calmed their rising excitement by saying in a gentle, friendly voice: "Why did you not speak to one of us, my child?"

And her mother controlled herself, and said quietly: "You know how much we think of our children, we who have lived such a lonely life; and—yes, we may say it, especially of you, Mildrid; for you have been so much to us."

Mildrid felt as if she did not know where she was.

"Yes, we did not think you would desert us like this."

It was her father who spoke last. Though the words came gently, they did not hurt the less.

"I will not desert you!" she stammered.

"You must not say that," he answered, more gravely than before, "for you have done it already."

Mildrid felt that this was true, and at the same time that it was not true, but she could not put her feeling into words.

Her mother went on: "Of what good has it all been, the love that we have shown our children, and the fear of God that we have taught them? In the first temptation—" for her daughter's sake she could say no more.

But Mildrid could bear it no longer. She threw her arms over the table, laid her head on them, her face towards her father, and sobbed.

Neither father nor mother was capable of adding by another reproachful word to the remorse she seemed to feel. So there was silence.

It might have lasted long—but Hans Haugen saw from where he sat that she was in need of help. His hunter's eye had caught every look, seen the movement of their lips, seen her silent struggle; now he saw her throw herself on the table, and he jumped up, and soon his light foot was heard in the passage. He knocked; they all looked up, but no one said, "Come in!" Mildrid half rose, blushing through her tears; the door opened, and Hans with his gun and dog stood there, pale but quite composed. He turned and shut the door, while the dog, wagging its tail, went up to Mildrid. Hans had been too preoccupied to notice that it had followed him in.

"Good morning!" said he. Mildrid fell back on her seat, drew a long breath, and looked at him with relief in her eyes; her fear, her bad conscience—all gone! *She was right, yes; she was right*—let come now whatever it pleased God to send!

No one had answered Hans's greeting, nor had he been asked to come forward.

"I am Hans Haugen," he said quietly; lowered his gun and stood holding it. After the parents had exchanged looks once or twice, he went on, but with a struggle: "I came down with Mildrid, for if she has done wrong, it was my fault."

Something had to be said. The mother looked at the father, and at last he said that all this had happened without their knowing anything of it, and that Mildrid could give them no explanation of how it had come about. Hans answered that neither could he. "I am not a boy," he said, "for I am twenty-eight; but yet it came this way, that I, who never cared for any one before, could think of nothing else in the world from the time I saw her. If she had said No—well, I can't tell—but I shouldn't have been good for much after that."

The quiet, straightforward way he said this made a good impression. Mildrid trembled; for she felt that this gave things a different look. Hans had his cap on, for in their district it was not the custom for a passer-by to take off his hat when he came in; but now he took it off unconsciously, hung it on the barrel of his gun, and crossed his hands over it. There was something about his whole appearance and behaviour that claimed consideration.

"Mildrid is so young," said her mother; "none of us had thought of anything like this beginning with her already."

"That is true enough, but to make up I am so much older," he answered; "and the housekeeping at home, in my house, is no great affair; it will not task her too hard—and I have plenty of help."

The parents looked at each other, at Mildrid, at him. "Do you mean her to go home with you?" the father asked incredulously, almost ironically.

"Yes," said Hans; "it is not the farm that I am coming after." He reddened, and so did Mildrid.

If the farm had sunk into the ground the parents could not have been more astonished than they were at hearing it thus despised, and Mildrid's silence showed that she agreed with Hans. There was something in this resolution of the young people, unintentional on their part, that, as it were, took away from the parents the right of decision; they felt themselves humbled.

"And it was you who said that you would not forsake us," said her mother in quiet reproach, that went to Mildrid's heart. But Hans came to her assistance:

"Every child that marries has to leave its parents."

He smiled, and added in a friendly way: "But it's not a long journey to Haugen from here—just a little over four miles."

Words are idle things at a time like this; thoughts take their own way in spite of them. The parents felt themselves deserted, almost deceived by the young ones. They knew that there was no fault to be found with the way of living at Haugen; the tourists had given the place a good name; from time to time it had been noticed in the newspapers; but Haugen was Haugen, and that their dearest child should wish to carry their race back to Haugen was more than they could bear! In such circumstances most people would likely have been angry, but what these two desired was to get quietly away from what pained them. They exchanged a look of understanding, and the father said mildly:

"This is too much for us all at once; we can't well give our answer yet."

"No," continued the mother; "we were not expecting such great news—nor to get it like this."

Hans stood quiet for a minute before he said:

"It is true enough that Mildrid should first have asked her parents' leave. But remember that neither of us knew what was happening till it was too late. For that is really the truth. Then we could do no more than come at once, both of us, and that we have done. You must not be too hard on us."

This left really nothing more to be said about their behaviour, and Hans's quiet manner made his words sound all the more trustworthy. Altogether Endrid felt that he was not holding his own against him, and the little confidence he had in himself made him the more desirous to get away.

"We do not know you," he said, and looked at his wife. "We must be allowed to think it over."

"Yes, that will certainly be best," went on Randi; "we ought to know something about the man we are to give our child to."

Mildrid felt the offence there was in these words, but looked imploringly at Hans.

"That is true," answered Hans, beginning to turn his gun under the one hand; "although I don't believe there are many men in the district much better known than I am. But perhaps some one has spoken ill of me?" He looked up to them.

Mildrid sat there feeling ashamed on her parents' account, and they themselves felt that they had perhaps awakened a false suspicion, and this they had no desire to do. So both said at once:

"No, we have heard nothing bad of you."

And the mother hastened to add that it was really the case that they hardly knew anything about him, for they had so seldom asked about the Haugen people. She meant no harm at all by saying this, and not till the words had passed her lips, did she notice that she had expressed herself unfortunately, and she could see that both her husband and Mildrid felt the same. It was a little time before the answer came:

"If the family of Tingvold have never asked after the Haugen people, the fault is not ours; we have been poor people till these last years."

In these few words lay a reproach that was felt by all three to be deserved, and that thoroughly. But never till now had it occurred to either husband or wife that they had been in this case neglecting a duty; never till now had they reflected that their poor relations at Haugen should not have been made to suffer for misfortunes of which they had been in no way the cause. They stole an awkward glance at each other, and sat still, feeling real shame. Hans had spoken quietly, though Randi's words must have been very irritating to him. This made both the old people feel that he was a fine fellow, and that they had two wrongs to make good again. Thus it came about that Endrid said:

"Let us take time and think things over; can't you stay here and have dinner with us? Then we can talk a little."

And Randi added: "Come away here and sit down."

Both of them rose.

Hans set away the gun with his cap on it, and went forward to the bench on which Mildrid was sitting, whereupon she at once got up, she did not know why. Her mother said she had things to see to in the kitchen, and went out. Her father was preparing to go too; but Mildrid did not wish to be alone with Hans as long as her parents withheld their consent, so she went towards the other door, and they presently saw her crossing the yard to her grandmother's house. As Endrid could not leave Hans alone, he turned and sat down again.

The two men talked together about indifferent matters—first it was about the hunting, about the Haugen brothers' arrangements in the little summer huts they had high up on the mountains, about the profits they made by this sort of thing, &c. &c. From this they came to Haugen itself, and the tourists, and the farm management; and from all he heard Endrid got the impression of there being prosperity there now, and plenty of life. Randi came backwards and forwards, making preparations for the dinner, and often listened to what was being said; and it was easy to see that the two old people, at first so shy of Hans, became by degrees a little surer of him; for the questions began to be more personal.

They did not fail to observe his good manners at the dinner-table. He sat with his back to the wall, opposite Mildrid and her mother; the father sat at the end of the table on his high seat. The farm people had dined earlier, in the kitchen, where indeed all in the house generally took their meals together. They were making the difference to-day because they were unwilling that Hans should be seen. Mildrid felt at table that her mother looked at her whenever Hans smiled. He had one of those serious faces that grow very pleasant when they smile. One or two such things Mildrid added together in her mind, and brought them to the sum she wanted to arrive at. Only she did not feel herself so sure, but that the strain in the room was too great for her, and she was glad enough to escape from it by going after dinner again to her grandmother's.

The men took a walk about the farm, but they neither went where the people were working, nor where grandmother could see them. Afterwards they came and sat in the room again, and now mother had finished her work and could sit with them. By degrees the conversation naturally became more confidential, and in course of time (but this was not till towards evening) Randi ventured to ask Hans how it had all come about between him and Mildrid; Mildrid herself had been able to give no account of it. Possibly it was principally out of feminine curiosity that the mother asked, but the question was a very welcome one to Hans.

He described everything minutely, and with such evident happiness, that the old people were almost at once carried away by his story. And when he came to yesterday—to the forced march Beret had made in search of him because Mildrid was plunged in anguish of mind on her parents' account—and then came to Mildrid herself, and told of her ever-increasing remorse because her parents knew nothing; told of her flight down to them, and how, worn-out in soul and body, she had had to sit down and rest and had fallen asleep, alone and unhappy—then the old people felt that they recognised their child again. And the mother especially began to feel that she had perhaps been too hard with her.

While the young man was telling about Mildrid, he was telling too, without being aware of it, about himself; for his love to Mildrid showed clearly in every word, and made her parents glad. He felt this himself at last, and was glad too—and the old couple, unaccustomed to such quiet self-reliance and strength, felt real happiness. This went on increasing, till the mother at last, without thinking, said smilingly:

"I suppose you've arranged everything right up to the wedding, you two—before asking either of us?"

The father laughed too, and Hans answered, just as it occurred to him at the moment, by softly singing a single line of the Wedding March,

"Play away! speed us on! we're in haste, I and you!"

and laughed; but was modest enough at once to turn to something else. He happened accidentally to look at Randi, and saw that she was quite pale. He felt in an instant that he had made a mistake in recalling that tune to her. Endrid looked apprehensively at his wife, whose emotion grew till it became so strong that she could not stay in the room; she got up and went out.

"I know I have done something wrong," said Hans anxiously.

Endrid made no reply. Hans, feeling very unhappy, got up to go after Randi and excuse himself, but sat down again, declaring that he had meant no harm at all.

"No, you could hardly be expected to understand rightly about that," said Endrid.

"Can't *you* go after her and put it right again!"

He had already such confidence in this man that he dared ask him anything.

But Endrid said: "No; rather leave her alone just now; I know her."

Hans, who a few minutes before had felt himself at the very goal of his desires, now felt himself cast into the depths of despair, and would not be cheered up, though Endrid strove patiently to do it. The dog helped by coming forward to them; for Endrid went on asking questions about him, and afterwards told with real pleasure about a dog he himself had had, and had taken much interest in, as is generally the way with people leading a lonely life.

Randi had gone out and sat down on the doorstep. The thought of her daughter's marriage and the sound of the Bridal March together had stirred up old memories too painfully. *She* had not, like her daughter, given herself willingly to a man she loved! The shame of her wedding-day had been deserved; and that shame, and the trouble, and the loss of their children—all the suffering and struggle of years came over her again.

And so all her Bible-reading and all her praying had been of no avail! She sat there in the most violent agitation! Her grief that she could thus be overcome caused her in despair to begin the bitterest self-accusation. Again she felt the scorn of the crowd at her foolish bridal procession; again she loathed herself for her own weakness—that she could not stop her crying then, nor her

41

thinking of it now—that with her want of self-control she had cast undeserved suspicion on her parents, destroyed her own health and through this caused the death of the children she bore, and lastly that with all this she had embittered the life of a loving husband, and feigned a piety that was not real, as her present behaviour clearly showed!

How dreadful that she still felt it in this way—that she had got no farther!

Then it burst upon her—both her crying in church and the consuming bitterness that had spoiled the early years of her married life had been *wounded vanity*. It was wounded vanity that was weeping now; and that might at any moment separate her from God, her happiness in this world and the world to come!

So worthless, so worthless did she feel herself that she dared not look up to God; for oh! how great were her shortcomings towards Him! But why, she began to wonder, why had she succumbed just now—at the moment when her daughter, in all true-heartedness and overflowing happiness, had given herself to the man she loved? Why at this moment arouse all the ugly memories and thoughts that lay dormant in her mind? Was she envious of Mildrid; envious of her own daughter? No, *that* she knew she was not—and she began to recover herself.

What a grand thought it was that her daughter was perhaps going to atone for *her* fault! Could children do that? Yes, as surely as they themselves were a work of ours, they could—but we must help too, with repentance, with gratitude! And before Randi knew what was happening, she could pray again, bowing in deep humility and contrition before the Lord, who had once more shown her what she was without Him. She prayed for grace as one that prays for life; for she felt that it was life that was coming to her again! Now her account was blotted out; it was just the last settling of it that had unnerved her.

She rose and looked up through streaming tears; she knew that things had come right now; there was One who had lifted the burden of pain from her!

Had she not had the same feeling often before? No, never a feeling like this—not till now was the victory won. And she went forward knowing that she had gained the mastery over herself. Something was broken that till now had bound her—she felt with every movement that she was free both in soul and body. And if, after God, she had her daughter to thank for this, that daughter should in return be helped to enjoy her own happiness to the full.

By this time she was in the passage of grandmother's house; but no one in the house recognised her step. She took hold of the latch and opened the door like a different person. "Mildrid, come here!" she said; and Mildrid and her grandmother looked at each other, for that was not mother. Mildrid ran to her. What could be happening? Her mother took her by the arm, shut the door behind her, so that they were alone, then threw her arms round her neck, and wept and wept, embracing her with a vehemence and happiness which Mildrid, uplifted by her love, could return right heartily.

"God for ever bless and recompense you!" whispered the mother.

The two sitting in the other house saw them coming across the yard, hand in hand, walking so fast that they felt sure something had happened. The door opened and both came forward. But instead of giving her to Hans, or saying anything to him or Endrid, the mother just put her arms once more round her daughter, and repeated with a fresh burst of emotion: "God for ever bless and reward you!"

Soon they were all sitting in grandmother's room. The old woman was very happy. She knew quite well who Hans Haugen was—the young people had often spoken about him; and she at once understood that this union wiped out, as it were, much that was painful in the life of her son and his wife. Besides, Hans's good looks rejoiced the cheery old woman's heart. They all stayed with her, and the day ended with father, after a psalm, reading from a prayer-book a portion beginning: "The Lord has been in our house!"

I shall only tell of two days in their life after this, and in each of these days only of a few minutes.

The first is the young people's wedding-day. Inga, Mildrid's cousin, herself a married woman now, had come to deck out the bride. This was done in the store-house. The old chest which held the family's bridal silver ornaments— crown, girdle, stomacher, brooches, rings—was drawn from its place. Grandmother had the key of it, and came to open it, Beret acting as her assistant. Mildrid had put on her wedding-dress and all the ornaments that belonged to herself, before this grandeur (well polished by Beret and grandmother the week before) came to light, glittering and heavy. One after another each ornament was tried. Beret held the mirror in front of the bride. Grandmother told how many of her family had worn these silver things on their wedding-day, the happiest of them all her own mother, Aslaug Haugen.

Presently they heard the Bridal March played outside; they all stopped, listened, and then hurried to the door to see what it meant. The first person they saw was Endrid, the bride's father. He had seen Hans Haugen with his brothers and sisters coming driving up the road to the farm. It was not often that any idea out of the common came to Endrid, but on this occasion it did occur to him that these guests ought to be received with the March of their race. He called out the fiddlers and started them; he was standing beside them himself, and some others had joined him, when Hans and his good brothers and sisters, in two carriages, drove into the yard. It was easily seen that this reception touched them.

An hour later the March of course struck up again. This was when the bride and bridegroom, and after them the bride's parents, came out, with the players going before them, to get into the carriages. At some great moments in our lives all the omens are propitious; to-day the bridal party drove away from Tingvold in glorious spring weather. The crowd at the church was so great that no one remembered having seen the like of it, on any occasion. And in this gathering each person knew the story of the family, and its connection with the Bridal March which was sounding exultantly in the sunshine over the heads of bride and bridegroom.

And because they were all thinking of the one thing, the pastor took a text for his address that allowed him to explain how our children are our life's crown, bearing clear witness to our honour, our development, our work.

On the way back from the altar Hans stopped just outside the church-door; he said something; the bride, in her superhuman happiness, did not hear it; but she felt what it was. He wished her to look at Ole Haugen's grave, how richly clad in flowers it lay to-day. She looked, and they passed out almost touching his headstone; the parents following them.

The other incident in their life that must be recalled is the visit of Endrid and Randi as grandparents. Hans had carried out his determination that they were to live at Haugen, although he had to promise that he would take Tingvold when the old people either could or would no longer manage it, and when the old grandmother was dead. But in their whole visit there is only one single thing that concerns us here, and that is that Randi, after a kind reception and good entertainment, when she was sitting with her daughter's child on her knee, began rocking it and crooning something—and what she crooned was the Bridal March. Her daughter clasped her hands in wonder and delight, but controlled herself at once and kept silence; Hans offered Endrid more to drink, which he declined; but this was on both sides only an excuse for exchanging a look.

FOOTNOTES:

[1] The old superstition that every man is followed by a "Vardöger" (an invisible animal, resembling him in character) is still common among the peasants.

ONE DAY

CHAPTER I

ELLA was generally known as the girl with the plait. But, thick as the plait was, if it had belonged to any one less shapely, less blonde, less sprightly, hardly any one would have noticed it; the merry life which it led behind her would have passed unobserved, and that, although it was the thickest plait which any one in the little town had ever boasted. Perhaps it looked even thicker than it really was, because Ella herself was little. It is not necessary to give its exact length, but it reached below her waist; a long way below it. Its colour was doubtful but inclined a little to red, though people in the town generally called it light, and we will accept their dictum without going into the question of half-tones. Her face was noticeable for its white skin, pretty shape, and classic profile; she had a small, full mouth, and eyes of unusual frankness, a trim little figure, but with rather short legs, so that in order to get over the ground as fast as it was her nature to do, her feet had to move very quickly. She was quick, indeed, in everything which she undertook, and that no doubt was why the plait was busier than plaits are wont to be.

Her mother was the widow of a government official, had a small fortune besides her pension, and lived in her own little house opposite the hotel close by the market. She was an unassuming woman, whose husband had influenced her in everything; he had been her pride, her light, and when she lost him, the object of her life was gone; she became absorbed in religion; but, as she was not dictatorial, she allowed her only child—who much resembled her father—to follow her own inclinations. The mother associated with no one except an elder sister, who owned a large farm near the town, but Ella was allowed to bring in her companions from school, boating, skating, and snow-shoeing; this, however, made no difference, for there was an instinctive prudence in her choice of friends; her liveliness was tempered by her mother's society and the quietness of the house. So that she was active and expeditious without being noisy, frank enough, but with self-command and heedfulness.

All the more strange, then, was an incident which occurred when she was between fourteen and fifteen. She had gone with a few friends to a concert which the Choral Society of the town, and one or two amateurs, were giving in aid of the Christmas charities. At this concert, Aksel Aarö sang Möhring's "Sleep in Peace." As every one knows, a subdued chorus carries the song forward; a flood of moonlight seemed to envelop it, and through it swept Aksel Aarö's voice. His voice was a clear, full, deep baritone, from which every one derived great pleasure. He could have drawn it out, without break or flaw, from here to Vienna. But within this voice Ella heard another, a simultaneous sound of weakness or pain, which she never doubted that everybody could hear. There was an emotion in its depths, an affecting confidence, which went to her heart; it seemed to say, "Sorrow, sorrow is the portion of my life; I cannot help myself, I am lost." Before she herself knew it, she was weeping bitterly. Anything more impressive than this voice she had never experienced. With every note her agitation increased, and she lost all control over herself.

Aarö was of moderate height, and slender, with a fair, silky beard, which hung down over his chest; his head was small, his eyes large and melancholy, with something in their depths which, like the voice, seemed to say "Sorrow, sorrow." This melancholy in the eyes she had noticed before, but had not fully understood it until now, when she heard his voice. Her tears would flow. But this would not do. She glanced quickly round; no one else was crying. She set her teeth, she pressed her arms against her sides, and her knees together till they ached and trembled. Why in the world should this happen to her and to no one else? She put her handkerchief to her lips, and forced herself to think of the beam of light which she had seen flash out from the lighthouse and disappear again, leaving the sea ghostly in the darkness. But no! her thoughts would return; they would not be controlled. Nothing could check the first sob, it would break out. Before all the astonished eyes she rose, left her seat, slipped quietly from the room and got away. No one came with her; no one dared to be seen near her.

You who read this, do you realise how dreadful it was? Have you been to such a—I had nearly written *silent*—concert, in a Norwegian coast town of somewhat pietist savour? Hardly any men are present. Either music is not to the masculine taste in the coast towns, or they are in some other part of the club, at billiards, or cards, or in the restaurant drinking punch, or reading the papers. Two or three perhaps have come up for a moment, and stand near the door, stand like those to whom the house belongs, and who wish to have a look at the strangers; or there really are one or two men sitting on the benches, squeezed in among the many coloured dresses, or else a few specimens are seen round the walls, like forgotten overcoats.

No! those who gather at the concerts are from the harems of the place; their elder inhabitants come to dream again, amidst beautiful words and touching music, of what they once persuaded themselves that they were, and what they had once believed was awaiting them. It is a harmless passing amusement. In the main they are better understood up above than here below, so that if a whiff of the kitchen or a few household worries do find their way into the dreams, it does not disturb them. The younger denizens of the harems dream that they *are* what the elders once believed themselves, and that *they* will attain at least to something of what the eldest have never reached. *They* had gained some information about life. In one thing old and young resemble each other; they are practical and prosperous by descent. They never allow their thoughts to stray very far. They know quite well that the glow which they feel as they listen to the words and music of great minds is not to be taken too seriously; it is only "What one always feels, you know."

When, therefore, one among them took this really seriously and began to cry about it, good gracious! In private it was called "foolery," in public "scandalous."

Ella had made a spectacle of herself. Her own dismay was immeasurable. No girl that she knew was less given to tears than herself; that she was certain of. She had as great a dread as any one of being looked at, or talked about. What in the world was it then? She was fond of music, certainly; she played herself, but she did not believe that she had any remarkable gift. Why, then, should she especially have been overcome by his song? What must he think of the silly girl? This thought troubled her most, and on this point she dare not confide in any one. Most people concluded that she had been ill, and she actually did keep indoors for a few days, and looked pale when she reappeared. Her friends teased her about it, but she let the matter drop.

In the winter there were several children's dances, one of which was at "Andresen's at the corner," and Ella was there. Just at the conclusion of the second quadrille, she heard whispered "Aksel Aarö, Aksel Aarö!" and there he stood at the door, with three other young fellows behind him. The hostess was his elder sister. The four had come up from a card party to look on.

Ella felt a thrill of delight, and at the same time her knees threatened to give way under her. She could neither see, nor understand clearly, but she felt great eyes on her. She was engrossed in a fold of her dress which did not hang properly, when he stood before her and said, "What a beautiful plait you have." His voice seemed to sprinkle it with gold-dust. He put out his hand as though he were going to touch it, but instead of doing so he stroked his beard. When he noticed her extreme timidity, he turned away. Several times during the evening she felt conscious of his presence; but he did not come up to her again.

The other men took part in the dancing, but Aarö did not dance. There was something about him which she thought specially charming; a reserved air of distinction, a polish in his address, a deference of that quiet kind which alone could have appealed to her. His walk gave the impression that he kept half his strength in reserve, and this was the same in everything. He was tall, but not broad-shouldered; the small, somewhat narrow head, set on a rather long neck. She had never before noticed the way in which he turned his head. She felt now that there could be something, yes, almost musical about it.

The room, and all that passed in it, seemed to float in light, but suddenly this light was gone. A little later she heard some one say, "Where is Aksel Aarö? Has he left?"

Aarö was not at home for very long that winter. He had already spent two years at Havre, from which place he had recently returned; he was now going for a couple of years to Hull. Before this, music had been a favourite pursuit with Ella; she had especially loved and studied harmony, but from this time forward she devoted herself to melody. All music had given her pleasure and she had made some progress in it; but now it became speech to her. She herself spoke in it or another spoke to her. Now, whoever she was with, there was always one as well, she was never alone now, not in the street, not at home; of this the plait was the sacred symbol.

In the course of the spring Fru Holmbo met Ella in the street as she was coming from the pastor's house with her prayer-book in her hand.

"Are you going to be confirmed?" asked Fru Holmbo.

"Yes."

"I have a message for you; can you guess from whom?"

Now, Fru Holmbo was a friend of Aksel Aarö's sister and very intimate with the family. Ella blushed and could not answer.

"I see that you know who it is from," said Fru Holmbo, and Ella blushed more than ever.

With a rather superior smile—and the prettiest lady in the town had a superabundance of them—she said, "Aksel Aarö is not fond of writing. We have only just received his first letter since he left; but in it he writes that when we see 'the girl with the plait,' we are to remember him to her.' She cried at Möhring's song; other people might have done so too,'" he wrote.

The tears sprang to Ella's eyes.

"No, no," said Fru Holmbo consolingly, "there is no harm in that."

CHAPTER II

Two years later, in the course of the winter, Ella was coming quickly up from the ice with her skates in her hand. She wore her new tight-fitting jacket for the first time; in fact, it was principally this jacket which had tempted her out.

The plait hung jauntily down from under her grey cap. It was longer and thicker than ever; it throve wonderfully.

As usual, she went round by "Andresen's at the corner." To see the house was enough. Just as her eyes rested on it, Aksel Aarö appeared in the doorway. He came slowly down the steps. He was at home again! His fair beard lay on the dark fur of his coat, a fur cap covered his low forehead and came down almost to his eyes; those large, attractive eyes. They looked at one another; they had to meet and pass; he smiled as he raised his cap, and she—stood still and curtseyed, like a schoolgirl in a short frock. For two years she had not dropped a curtsey, or done otherwise than bow like a grown-up person. Short people are most particular about this privilege; but to him, before whom she specially wished to appear grown-up, she had stood still and curtseyed as when he had last seen her. Occupied by this mishap she rushed into another. She said to herself, "Do not look round, keep yourself stiff, do not look round; do you hear?" But at the corner, just as she was turning away from him, she did look back for all that, and saw him do the same. From that moment there were no other people, no houses, no time or place. She did not know how she got home, or why she lay crying on her bed, with her face in the pillow.

A fortnight later, there was a large party at the club, in honour of Aksel Aarö. Every one wished to be there, every one wished to bid their popular friend welcome home. He had been greatly missed. They had heard from Hull how indispensable he had by degrees become in society there. If his voice had had a greater compass—it did not comprise a large range of notes—he would have obtained an engagement at Her Majesty's Theatre; so it was said over there. At this ball, the Choral Society—his old Choral Society—would again sing with him.

Ella was there; she came too early—only four people before her. She trembled with expectancy in the empty rooms and passages, but more especially in the hall where she had made "a spectacle of herself." She wore a red ball-dress, without any ornaments or flowers; this was by her mother's wish. She feared that she had betrayed herself by coming so early, and remained alone in a side room; she did not appear until the rooms had been fully lighted, and the perfume, the buzz of voices, and the tuning of instruments lured her in. Ella was so short, that when she came into the crowd, she had not seen Aksel Aarö when she heard several whispers of "There he is," and some one added, "He is coming towards us." It was Fru Holmbo for whom he was looking, and to whom he bowed; but just behind her stood Ella. When she felt that she was discovered, the bud blushed rosier than its calyx. He left Fru Holmbo at once.

"Good evening," he said very softly, holding out his hand, which Ella took without looking up. "Good evening," he said again, still more softly, and drew nearer.

She was aware of a gentle pressure and had to raise her eyes. They conveyed a bashful message half confident, half timid. It was a rapid glance, by which no one was enlightened or scandalised. He looked down at her, while he stroked his beard, but either because he had nothing more to say—he was not talkative—or that he could not say what he wished; he became absolutely silent. In the quiet way which was peculiar to him he turned and left her. He was on at once by his friends, and for the rest of the evening she only saw him now and again, and always at a distance.

He did not dance, but she did. Everybody said how "sweet" she was (it was said with all respect); and that evening she really did beam with happiness. In whatever part of the room Aksel Aarö chanced to be, she felt conscious of his presence, felt a secret delight in whirling past him. His eyes followed her, his nearness made all and everything resplendent.

Standing in the doorway was a heavy, sturdy fellow, who had constituted himself the critic of the assemblage. He appeared to be between thirty and forty; nearer the latter; he had a weather-beaten, coarsely-moulded, but spirited face, black hair, and hazel eyes; his figure approached the gigantic. Every one in the room knew him; Hjalmar Olsen, the fearless commander of one of the largest steamers.

He scanned the dancers as they passed him, but gave the palm to the little one in the red dress; she was the pleasantest to look at: not only was she a fine girl, but her buoyant happiness seemed to infect him. When Aksel Aarö approached, Hjalmar Olsen received a share of the love glances which streamed from her eyes. She danced every dance. Hjalmar Olsen was tall enough to catch glimpses of her in all parts of the room. She also noticed him; he soon became a lighthouse in her voyage, but a lighthouse which interested itself in the ships. Thus he now felt that she was in danger so near to Peter Klausson's waistcoat. He knew Peter Klausson.

Her tiny feet tripped a waltz, while the plait kept up an accompanying polka. Certainly Peter Klausson did press her too close to his waistcoat!

Olsen therefore sought her out as soon as the waltz was over, but it was not so easy to secure a dance; a waltz was the first one for which she was free, and she gave him that. Just as this was arranged, every one pressed towards the platform, on which the Choral Society now appeared. Ella felt herself hopelessly little when they all rushed forward and packed themselves together. Hjalmar Olsen, who saw her vain attempts to obtain a peep, offered to lift her up on to the bench which ran along the wall, by which they were standing. She dare not agree to this, but he saw that others were mounting the bench, and before she could prevent it, she was up there too. Almost at the same moment Aksel Aarö came in among his companions and was received with the most energetic hand-clapping by all his friends—men as well as women. He bowed politely though somewhat coldly, but the expressions of welcome did not cease until his companions drew back a little, while he came forward. First of all, the Society gave one of its older songs. He kept his voice on a level with the others, which was considered in very good taste. After this the conductor took his seat at the piano, to accompany a song which Aarö wished to give alone. The song was a composition of Selmer and much in fashion at the capital. It could be sung by men as well as women, only in the last verse *her* had to be substituted for *his*. Here it had never been heard before.

During the first song Aarö had searched the room with his eyes, and, from the moment when he discovered where Ella stood, he had kept them fixed there. Now he placed himself near the piano, and during the song he continued to look in her direction. As he sang, his melancholy eyes lighted up; his figure grew plastic.

> I sing to one, to only one
>   Of all the listening throng;
> To one alone is fully known
>   The meaning of my song.
> Lend power, ye listeners, to each word.
>   But for that only one
> Who in me woke sweet music's chord
>   My song had ne'er been sung.
>
> Though deviously the path may run,
>   Passing through all hearts here,
> Yet still is it the only one
>   Which to one heart is near.
> Strengthen, oh, loving hearts, my song,
>   So that it still may swell
> Through all love's choir; the only one
>   That in her heart may dwell.

His voice was captivating; no one had ever listened to such a love-message. This time many beside Ella had tears in their eyes. When the song ended, they all remained waiting for some moments, as though expecting another verse; and there was a short silence, but then applause broke forth such as had never been heard. They wanted to have the song again, but no one had yet known Aksel Aarö to sing anything twice running; so they relinquished the idea.

Ella had never heard the song; neither words nor music. When, with his eyes turned in her direction, he had begun to sing, she felt as though she should fall; such unheard-of boldness she had never imagined. That he, otherwise so considerate, should sing this across to her, so that all could hear! White as the wall against which she leaned for support, she suffered such anguish of mind, that she looked round for help. Immediately behind her, on the same bench, stood Fru Holmbo, magnetised, beautiful as a statue. She no more saw Ella's distress than she did the clock in the market-place. This absolute indifference calmed her, she recovered her self-possession. The neighbourhood of the others, which had been so terrible to her, was of no consequence, so long as they did not perceive anything. She could listen now without distress. More covertly, more charmingly, he could not have spoken, notwithstanding that every one heard it. If only he had not looked at her! If only she had been able to hide herself!

As soon as the last notes ceased, she jumped down from the bench. Among all the shoulders her shyness returned—her happy dream, her secret in its bridal attire. What was it that had happened? What would happen next? All round her were sparkling eyes, applauding voices, clapping hands—was it not as though they lighted torches in his honour, paid him homage—was not all this in her honour as well?

Dancing began again at once, and off she went. Off as though all were done for her, or as though she were the "only one!" Her partners tried, one after another, to talk to her, but in vain. She only laughed, laughed in their faces, as though they were mad, and she alone understood the state of the case.

She danced, beamed, laughed, from one partner to another. So when Olsen got his waltz it was as though he were received with a score of fresh bouquets and a "Long live Hjalmar Olsen!" He was more than flattered. When she laid her white arm on his black coat he felt that at the bottom he was as unworthy as Peter Klausson. He certainly would not sully her, he held her punctiliously away from him. When he fancied that she was laughing, and wished to see the little creature's merry face, down there near his waistcoat, and in the endeavour to do so, thought that he had been indiscreet, Hjalmar Olsen felt ashamed of himself, and danced on with his eyes staring straight before him, like a sleep-walker. He danced on in a dream of self-satisfaction and transport. Ella tried now and then to touch the floor; she wished to have at least some certainty that she was keeping time. Impossible! He took charge at once, of himself, her dance and his, her time and his, she never got near the floor without an effort, all the rest was an aerial flight. He could hear her laughing and was pleased that she was enjoying it, but he did not look at her. Those with whom he came into collision were less pleased, which was *their* affair. He was greatly put out when the music ceased; they were only just getting into swing, but he was obliged to put her down at the compulsory stopping-place.

Shortly afterwards there was some more singing, first by the Society alone, then they and Aarö together sang Grieg's "Landfall." Finally, Aarö sang to a piano accompaniment. This time Ella had hidden herself among those at the back, but as they constantly pressed forward she remained standing alone. This exactly suited her; she saw him, but he did not see her, nor even look towards the place where she was standing.

She had never heard this song, did not even know that it existed, although when the first words were heard it was evident that it was known to the others. Of course she knew that each word and note were his, but as he had before chosen a story which would only reach the one to whom he wished to sing, she did not doubt that it was the same now. The first words, "My young love's veiled," could there be a truer picture of concealed love? Once more it was for her! That the veil should be lifted but for him and dropped as soon as any one else could see. Was not that as it must be between them? That love's secrecy is like a sacred place, that in it is hidden earth's highest happiness. She trembled as she recognised it. The music swept the words over her like ice-cold water, this perfect comprehension made her shiver, with fear and joy at the same time. No one saw her, that was her safeguard. She dreaded every fresh word before it came, and each one again made her shiver. With her arms pressed against her breast, her head bowed over her hands, she stood and trembled as though waves surged over her. And when the second verse came with the line, "The greatest joy this world can give," and especially when it was repeated, her tears would well forth, as they had done once before. She checked them with all her might, but remembering how little it had helped her then, her powers of resistance gave way, she was almost sobbing when the very word was used in the song. The coincidence was too superb, it swept all emotion aside, she could have laughed aloud instead. She was sure of everything, everything now. It thus happened that the last line in its literal sense, in its jubilant sympathy, came to her like a flash of lightning, like the stab of a knife. The song ran thus:

> My young love's veiled to all but me,
> No eyes save mine those eyes may see,
> > Which, while to others all unknown,
> > Command, melt, beam for me alone.
> Down falls the veil, would others see.
>
> In every good, where two are one,
> A twofold holiness doth reign;
> > The greatest joy this world can give

Is when earth's long desires shall live,
When two as soul to soul are born again.

Why must my love then veiled be?
Why sobs she piteous, silently,
    As though her heart must break for love?
    Because that veil from pain is wove,
And all our joy in yearning need we see.

Startling, deafening applause! They must, they would have the song again, this time Aarö's haughty opposition should be useless; but he would not give way, and at last some of the audience gave up the attempt, though others continued insistent.

During this interval several ladies escaped out of the crowd: they passed near Ella.

"Did you see Fru Holmbo, how she hid herself and cried?"

"Yes, but did you see her during the first song? Up on the bench? It was to her that he was singing the whole time."

Not long afterwards—it might have been about two in the morning—a little cloaked figure flew along the streets. By her hood and wraps the watchman judged that she must be one of the ladies from the ball. They generally had some one with them, but the ball was not over yet. Something had evidently happened; she was going so quickly too.

It was Ella. She passed near the deserted Town Hall, which was now used as a warehouse. The outer walls still remained, but the beautiful interior wood-work had been sold and removed. That is how it is with me, thought Ella. She flew along as fast as she could, onward to sleepless nights and joyless days.

In the course of the morning Aksel Aarö was carried home by his companions, dead drunk. By some it was maintained that he had swallowed a tumbler of whisky in the belief that it was beer; others said that he was a "bout drinker." He had long been so but had concealed it. Those are called "bout-drinkers" who at long intervals seem impelled to drink. His father had been so before him.

A few days later Aksel Aarö went quietly off to America.

CHAPTER III

ANOTHER of those who had been at the ball, steamed about the same time across the Atlantic. This was Hjalmar Olsen.

His ship experienced a continuous northwesterly gale, and the harder it blew, the more grog he drank; but as he did so he was astonished to find that a memory of the ball constantly rose before him—the little rosy red one; the girl with the plait. Hjalmar Olsen was of opinion that he had conducted himself in a very gentleman-like manner towards her. At first this did not very much occupy his thoughts; he had been twice engaged already, and each time it had been broken off. If he engaged himself a third time he must marry at once. He had formed this determination often before, but he did not really think very seriously about it.

A steamer is not many days between ports, and at each there is plenty of amusement. He went to New York, from there to New Orleans, thence to Brazil and back, once again to Brazil, finally returning direct to England and Norway. But often during the voyage, and especially over a glass of punch, he recalled the girl with the plait. How she had looked at him. It did him good only to think of it. He was not very fond of letter-writing, or perhaps he would have written to her. But when he arrived at Christiania, and heard from a friend that her mother was dying, he thought at once: "I shall certainly go and see her; she will think it very good of me, if I do so just now."

Two days later he was sitting before her in the parlour of the little house near the hotel and market-place. His large hands, black with hair and sunburn, stroked his knees as he stooped smilingly forward and asked if she would have him.

She sat lower than he did; her full figure and plump arms were set off by a brown dress, which he stared down on when he did not look into her pale face. She felt each movement of his eyes. She had come from the other room, and from thoughts of death; she heard a little cuckoo clock upstairs announce that it was seven o'clock, and the little thing reminded her of all that was now past. One thing with another made her turn from him with tears in her eyes as she said, "I cannot possibly think of such things how." She rose and walked towards her flowers in the window.

He was obliged to rise also. "Perhaps she will answer me presently," he thought; and this belief gave him words, awkward perhaps, but fairly plain.

She only shook her head and did not look up.

He walked off in a rage, and when he turned and looked at the house again—the little doll's house—he longed to throw it bodily into the sea.

He spent the evening, while waiting for the steamer to Christiania, with Peter Klausson and a few friends, and it was not long before they discovered on what errand he had been, and how he had sped. They knew, too, how he had fared on former occasions. The amount which Hjalmar Olsen drank was in proportion to his chagrin; and the next morning he awoke on board the steamer in a deplorable condition.

Not long afterwards Ella received a well-written letter of excuse, in which he explained that his coming at that time had been well meant, and that it was only when he was there that he realised how foolish it had been. She must not be vexed with him for it. In the course of a month she again received a letter. He hoped that she had forgiven him; he for his part could not forget her. There was nothing more added. Ella was pleased with both the letters. They were well expressed and they showed constancy; but it never occurred to her for a moment that this indirect offer could be received in any other way than before.

She had gone to Christiania in order to perfect herself in the piano and in book-keeping. She added the latter because she had always had a turn for arithmetic. She felt altogether unsettled. Her mother was dead; she had inherited the house and a small fortune, and she wanted to try and help herself. She did not associate with any one in the strange town. She was used to dreaming and making plans without a confidant.

From Aksel Aarö came wonderful tidings. After he had sung before a large party in New York a wealthy old man had invited him to come and see him, and since then they had lived together like father and son. So the story ran in the town long before there came a letter from Aarö himself; but when it arrived, it entirely confirmed the rumour. It was after this that Ella received a third letter from Hjalmar Olsen. He asked in respectful terms if she would take it amiss if he were to pay her a visit when he came home: he knew where she was living. Before she had arrived at a conclusion as to how she should answer, a paragraph appeared in all the Norwegian papers, copied from the American ones, giving an account of how Hjalmar Olsen, in the teeth of a gale, and at the risk of his own ship, had saved the passengers and crew of an ocean steamer, the propeller of which had been injured off the American coast. Two steamers had passed without daring to render assistance, the weather was so terrific. Olsen had remained by the vessel for twenty-four hours. It was a wonderful deed which he had done. In New York, and subsequently when he arrived in Liverpool, he had been fêted at the Sailors' Clubs, and been presented with medals and addresses. When he arrived in Christiania, he was received with the highest honours. Big and burly as he was, he easily obtained the homage of the populace: they always love large print.

In the midst of all this he sought out Ella. She had hidden herself away; she had but a poor opinion of herself since her discomfiture. In her imagination he had assumed almost unnatural proportions, and when he came and took her out with him, she felt as though she had once more exchanged the close atmosphere of the house for free air and sunshine. She even felt something of her old self-confidence. His feelings for her were the same; that she noticed at once, as she studied him. He knew the forms of society, and could pay attention and render homage with dignity; he refrained from any premature speech. She had heard that he was prone to take a glass too much, but she saw nothing in that. A handsome fellow, a man such as one seldom sees, a little weather-beaten perhaps, but most sailors are the same. Something undefined in his eyes frightened her, as did his greediness at table. Sometimes she was startled at the vehemence of his opinions. If only she had been at home, and could have made inquiries beforehand! But he was to leave very soon, and had said jestingly that the next time that he proposed, he would be betrothed and married all at once. This plain-speaking and precipitation pleased her, not less than his energy and authoritative manner, although she felt frightened— frightened, and at the same time flattered, that so much energy and authoritativeness should bow before her, and that at a time when all paid court to him.

Then an idea, which she thought very sensible, occurred to her. She would, in the event of an offer, impose two conditions: she must retain the control of her own property, and never be forced to accompany him on his voyages. In case his energy and tone of authority should chance to become intractable a limit was thus set, and she would, from the outset, make him comprehend that, little as she was, she knew how to protect both herself and her possessions.

When the offer came—it was made in a box at the theatre—she had not courage sufficient to make her stipulation. His expression filled her with horror—for the first time. She often thought of it afterwards. Instead of acting upon this intuitive perception, she began to speculate on what would happen if she were again to say No! She had accepted his friendship although she knew what was coming. The conditions, the conditions—they should settle it! If he accepted them, it should be as he wished, and then there could be no possible danger. So she wrote and propounded them.

He came the next day and asked for the necessary papers, so that he could himself arrange both about the property and the contract. He evidently looked upon it as a matter of business, and seemed thoroughly pleased.

Three days later they were married. It was an imposing ceremony, and there was a large concourse; it had been announced in all the papers.

Demonstrations of admiration and respect followed, much parade and many speeches, mingled with witticisms over his size and her smallness. This lasted from five in the evening till after midnight, in rather mixed company. As time wore on, and the champagne continually flowed, many of the guests became boisterous and somewhat intrusive, and among them the bridegroom.

The next morning, at seven o'clock, Ella sat dressed and alone, in a room next to their bedroom, the door of which stood open. From it she could hear her husband's snores. She sat there still and deadly pale, without tears and without feeling. She divided the occurrences into two—what had happened and what had been said; what had been said and what had happened: she did not know which was the worst. This man's longing had been inflamed by deadly hate. From the time that she had said No! he had made it the object of his life to force her to say Yes! He told her that she should pay for having nearly made him ridiculous a third time. She should pay for it all—she, who had dared to make insulting conditions. He would break the neck of her conditions like a shrimp. Let her try to refuse to go on board with him, or attempt to control anything herself.

Then that which had happened. A fly caught in a spider's web, that was what she thought of.

But had she not experienced such a feeling once before? O God, the night of the ball! She had a vague feeling that that night had fore-doomed her to this; but she could not make it clear to herself. On the other hand, she asked herself if what we fail in has not a greater influence on our lives than that which we succeed in.

Three or four hours after this, Hjalmar Olsen sat at the breakfast-table; he was dull and silent, but perfectly polite, as though nothing had happened. Perhaps he had been too drunk to be quite accountable, or it might be that his politeness was calculated with the hope of inducing her to come with him and visit his ship. He asked her to do so, as he left the table, but neither promises nor threats could induce her to go on board even for the shortest time. Her terror saved her.

Some months later an announcement appeared in the papers that she wished to take pupils both for the piano and book-keeping. She was once more living in her own little house in her native town. She was at this time enciente.

One day an old friend of Aksel Aarö's came to see her; he was to remember Aarö very kindly to her, and to congratulate her on her marriage. She controlled her rising emotion, and asked quietly how he was getting on. Most wonderfully; he was still living with the same old man, to whom, by degrees, he had entirely devoted himself. This was the very thing for Aarö: it suited him to devote himself completely to one person. He had gone through a course of treatment for his inherited failing and believed himself to be cured.

"And how is Fru Holmbo?" asked Ella. She was frightened when she had said it, but she felt an intense bitterness which would break out. She had noticed how thin and pale Fru Holmbo looked—she evidently missed Aarö, and that was too much!

The friend smiled: "Oh! have you heard that silly rumour? No, Aksel Aarö was only the medium between her and the man to whom she was secretly attached. The two friends had lived together abroad. Some months ago there had been a talk about a business journey to Copenhagen, and Fru Holmbo went there also. But there had undoubtedly been something between them for a long time."

That night Ella wept for a long time before she fell asleep. She lay and stroked her plait, which she had drawn on to her bosom. She had often thought of cutting it off, but it was still there.

CHAPTER IV

In the course of the two first years of her marriage she had two children. Whenever she was alone, she divided her time between them and her teaching. Her husband hardly contributed anything to the household, except during the brief periods that he passed at home, and then the money was squandered in the extravagant life which he led with his companions. During these visits the "young ones" were sent off to their aunt. "One could not take four steps without going through the walls of this wretched little house," he said. At these times she also gave up the lessons; she had no time for anything except to wait on him.

Every one realised that she could not be happy, but no one suspected that her whole life was one of dread—dread of the telegram which would announce his coming, if only for a few days, dread of what might happen when he came. When he was there she never attempted to oppose him, but displayed to him, and every one else, those frank eyes and quick, but quiet, ways which enabled her to come and go without being noticed. When he was gone, she would suddenly collapse, and, worn out with the strain of days and nights, be obliged to take to her bed.

Each time that he came home he kept less guard over himself, and was more careless as regarded others. Had she known that men who have expended their strength as he had done are as a rule worn out at forty—and many such are to be found in the coast-towns—she would have understood that these very things were signs of failure. He had advanced far along the road. To her he only appeared more and more disgusting. He was but little at home, which helped her. She had determined that she and her boys should live in the best manner, and this again was a help to her; but more than all was her constant employment and the regard which every one felt for her. After five years of marriage she looked as charming as ever, and appeared as cheerful and lively; she was accustomed to conceal her feelings.

Her children were now—the elder four, the second three years old. They were rarely seen anywhere but in the market-place, on the snow-heaps in winter and on the sand-heaps in summer, or else they were in the country with their aunt whom they had adopted as "grandmother."

Next to the care of the little boys, flowers were Ella's greatest delight. She had a great many, which made the house appear smaller than it really was. She could play with the boys, but she could share her thoughts with the flowers. When she watered them, she felt acutely how much she suffered. When she dried their leaves, she longed for pleasant words and kindly eyes. When she removed dead twigs and superfluous shoots, when she re-potted them, she often cried with longing; the thought that there was no one to care for her overcame her.

Five years were gone, then, when one day it was reported through the whole town that Aksel Aarö had become a rich man. His old friend was dead and had left him a large annuity. It was also said that he had been a second time treated for dypsomania. The previous treatment had not been successful, but he was now cured. One could see how popular Aarö was, for there was hardly anybody who was not pleased.

On Wednesday the 16th of March, 1892, at four o'clock in the afternoon, Ella sat at work near her flowers; from there she could see the hotel. At the corner window in the second story stood the man of whom she was thinking—stood and looked down at her.

She got up and he bowed twice. She remained standing as he crossed the market-place. He wore a dark fur cap, and his fair beard hung down over his black silk waistcoat. His face was rather pale, but there was a brighter expression in his eyes. He knocked, she could not speak or move, but when he opened the door and came into the room, she sank into a chair and wept. He came slowly forward, took a chair and sat down near her. "You must not be frightened because I came straight to you, it is such a pleasure to see you again." Ah! how they sounded in this house, those few words full of consideration and confidence. He had acquired a foreign accent, but the voice, the voice! And he did not misconstrue her weakness, but tried to help her. By degrees she became her old self, confiding, bright, timid.

"It was so entirely unexpected," she said.

"All that has occurred in the meantime rushes in on one," he added courteously.

Not much more was said. He was preparing to leave, when his brother-in-law entered. Aarö looked at her boys out on the snow-heap, he looked at her flowers, her piano, her music, then asked if he might come again. He had been there hardly five minutes, but an impression rested on her mind somewhat as the magnificent fair beard rested on the silk waistcoat. The room was hallowed, the piano, the music, the chair on which he had sat, even the carpet on which he had walked—in his very walk there was consideration for her. She felt that all that he had said and done showed sympathy for her fate. She could do nothing more that day, she hardly slept during the night, but the change which had taken place in her was nothing less than the bringing of something into the daylight again from five years ago, from six years indeed, as one brings flowers out of the cellar, where they have been put for their winter sleep, up into the spring-time again. As this thought passed through her mind, she made the same gesture at least twenty times, she laid both hands on her breast, one over the other, as though to control it: it must not speak too loudly.

The next day their conversation flowed more freely. The children were called in. After looking at them for a while, he said: "You have something real there."

In a little time they were such good friends, he and the boys, that he was down on all-fours playing horses with them, and did some quite new tricks which they thought extremely amusing; he then invited them to come for a drive the next day. After a thaw, there had been an unusually heavy fall of snow; the town was white and the state of the roads perfect.

Before he left Ella offered to brush him; the carpet had not been as well swept as it should have been. He took the clothes-brush from her and used it himself, but he had unfortunately lain on his back as well, so she was obliged to help him. She brushed his coat lightly and deftly, but she was never satisfied, nor was he yet properly brushed in front. He had to do it over again: she stood and looked on. When he had finished she took the brush into the kitchen.

"How funny that you should still wear your plait," said he, as she went out. She remained away for some time, and came in again by another door. He had gone. The children said that some one had come across for him.

The next morning the little boys had their drive. They did not return until late in the afternoon. They had been to Baadshaug, a watering-place with an hotel and an excellent restaurant, to which people were very fond of making excursions during the winter. His sister's youngest boy was with them, and while all three went back with the horses to "Andresen's at the corner," Aarö remained standing in the passage. Never had Ella seen him so cheerful. His eyes sparkled, and he talked from the time he came to the time he left. He talked about the Norwegian winter which he had never realised before; how could that have been? For many years he had had in his *répertoire* a song in praise of winter, the old winter song which she knew as well: "Summer sleeps in winter's arms"—yes, she knew it—and he only now realised how true it was. The influence of winter on people's lives must be immense; why it was nearly half their lives; what health and beauty and what power of imagination it must give. He began to describe what he had seen in the woods that day. He did not use many words, but he gave a clear picture; he talked till he became quite excited, and looked at her the whole time with a rapturous expression.

It was but for a few moments. He stood there muffled in furs: but when he had gone it seemed to her that she had never truly seen him before. He was an enthusiast then—an enthusiast whose depths never revealed themselves. Was his singing a message from this enthusiasm? Was this why his voice carried everybody away with it into another region? That melancholy father of his, when a craving for drink seized him, would shut himself up with his violin, and play and play till he became helpless. Had the son, too, this dislike of companionship, this delight in his own enthusiasm? God be praised, Aksel Aarö was saved! Was it not from the depths of his enthusiasm that he had looked at her? This forced itself upon her for the first time; she had been occupied before by the change in him, but now it forced itself upon her— hotly, with a thrill of fear and joy. A message of gladness which still quivered with doubt. Was the decisive moment of her life approaching? She felt that she coloured. She could not remain quiet; she went to the window to look for him; then paced the room, trying to discover what she might believe. All his words, his looks, his gestures, since he had first come there, rose before her. But he had been reserved, almost niggardly, with them. But that was just their charm. His eyes had now interpreted them, and those eyes enveloped her; she gave herself absolutely up to them.

Her servant brought in a letter; it was a Christmas card, in an envelope without a direction, from Aksel Aarö—one of the usual Christmas cards, representing a number of young people in snow-shoes. Below was printed:

Winter white,
Has roses red.

On the other side, in a clear round hand, "In the woods to-day I could not but think of you. A. A.." That was all.

"That is like him, he says nothing more. When he passes a shop-window in which he sees such a card, he thinks of me; and not only does he think of me but he sends me his thoughts." Or was she mistaken. Ella was diffident; surely this could not be misconstrued. The Christmas card—was it not a harbinger? The two young couples on it and the words—surely he meant something by that. His enraptured eyes again rose before her; they seemed not only to envelop her, but to caress her. She thought neither of past nor future; she lived only in the present. She lay wide awake that night looking at the moonlight. Now, now, now, was whispered. Had she but clung to the dream of her life, even when the reality had seemed so cruel, she would have held her own; because she had been uncertain about it, all had become uncertain. But the greater the suffering had been, the greater, perhaps, would be the bliss. She fell asleep in the soft white light, which she took with her into her dreams. She woke among light, bright clouds, which gathered round the glittering thought of what might be awaiting her to-day. He had not said a word. This bashfulness was what she loved the best of anything in him. It was just that which was the surest pledge. It would be to-day.

CHAPTER V

SHE took a long time over her bath, an almost longer time in doing her hair; out of the chest of drawers, which she had used as a child, and which still stood in its old place—out of its lowest drawer she took her finest underlinen. She had never worn it but once—on her wedding-day—before the desecration, never since. But to-day—Now, now, now! Not one garment which she put on had ever been touched by any one but herself. She wished to be what she had been in her dreams.

She went to the children, who were awake but not dressed.

"Listen, boys! To-day Tea shall take you to see grandmother."

Great delight, shared by Tea, for this meant a holiday.

"Mamma, mamma!" she heard behind her, as she ran down to the kitchen to get a cup of coffee, and then she was off. First she must get some flowers, then put off her lessons. For now, now, now!

Out in the street she remembered that it was too early to get anything, so she went for a walk, beyond the town, the freshest, the brightest, that she had ever taken. She came back again just as Fru Holmbo was opening her shop. As Ella entered the "flower-woman" was holding an expensive bouquet in her hand, ready to be sent out.

"I will have that!" cried Ella, shutting the door behind her.

"You!" said Fru Holmbo a little doubtfully; the bouquet was a very expensive one.

"Yes, I must have it;" Ella's little green purse was ready. The bouquet had been ordered for the best house in the town, and Fru Holmbo said so.

"That does not matter," answered Ella. Such genuine admiration of a bouquet had never been seen—and Ella got it.

From there she went to "Andresen's at the corner." One of the shopmen took lessons in book-keeping from her. She wished to put him off, and asked him to tell the whole of the large class. She asked him this with kindling eyes, and he gladly promised to do so. The daintiest red shawl was hanging just before her. She must have it to wear over her head to-day when she drove out; for that she would drive to-day there was no doubt. Andresen himself came up, just as she was asking about the shawl. He caught a glimpse of her bouquet, under the paper. "Those are lovely roses," he said. She took one out at once, and gave it to him. From the rose he looked at her; she laughed and asked if he would take a little off the price of the shawl; she had not quite enough money left.

"How much have you?" he asked.

"Just half a krone too little," she replied.

He himself wrapped up the shawl for her. In the street she met Cecilie Monrad, whose sister studied music with Ella; she was thus saved a walk to the other end of the town to put her off. "Everything favours me to-day," she thought.

"Did you see about those two who committed suicide together at Copenhagen?" asked Cecilie.

"Yes, she had." Fröken Monrad thought that it was horrible.

"Why?"

"Why the man was married!"

"True enough," answered Ella, "but they loved each other." Her eyes glowed; Cecilie lowered hers and blushed. Ella took her hand and pressed it. "I tumbled into a love-story there," she thought, and flew, rather than walked, up to the villas, where most of her pupils lived. On a roof she saw two starlings; the first that year. The thaw of a few days back had deceived them. Not that the starlings were dispirited. No, they loved! "Mamma, mamma," she seemed to hear at the same moment. It was certainly her boys; she had thought of them when she saw the starlings. She was so occupied with this that she walked right across to the side of the road and trod on a piece of board, which tilted up and nearly threw her down; but under the board Spring reigned. They had come with the thaw, they were certainly dandelions! However ugly they may be in the summer, the first ones are always welcome. She stooped down and gathered the flowers; she put them with the roses. The dandelions looked very shabby there, but they were the first this year, and found to-day!

After this she was absolutely boisterous. She skipped down the hills when her errand was finished. She greeted friends and mere acquaintance alike, and when she again saw Cecilie she put down the flowers, made a snowball, and threw it at her back.

When she got home she wrapped the children well up and put them into the sledge with Tea. "Mamma, mamma!" they shouted and pointed up towards the hotel. There stood Aksel Aarö. He bowed to her.

Soon afterwards he came across. "You are quite alone," he said as he entered.

"Yes." She was arranging the flowers and did not look up for she was trembling.

"Is it a birthday to-day?" he asked.

"Do you mean because of the flowers?"

"Yes. What lovely roses, and those in the glass—dandelions?"

"The first this year," she answered.

He did not look at them. He stood and fidgeted, as though he were thinking of something.

"May I sing to you?" He said at last.

"Yes, indeed." She left the flowers, in order to open the piano and screw down the music-stool, and then drew quietly back.

After a long and subdued prelude, he began with the "Sunset Song," by Ole Olsen, very softly, as he had spoken and moved ever since he came in. Never had he sung more beautifully; he had greatly improved, but the voice was the same, nay, there was even more despair and suffering in it than when she had heard it for the first time. "Sorrow, sorrow, oh, I am lost!" She heard it again plainly. At the end of the first verse, she sat bending forward, and weeping bitterly. She had not even tried to control herself. He heard her and turned round, a moment afterwards she felt him approach her, it even seemed to her that he kissed her plait, certainly he had bent down over her, for she could feel his breath. But she did not raise her head, she dare not.

He walked across the room, returned and then walked back again. Her agitation subsided, she sat immovable and waited.

"May I be allowed to take you for a drive to-day?" she heard him say.

She had known the whole morning that they would go for a drive together, so she was not surprised. Just as *that* had now been fulfilled, so would the other be—everything. She looked up through her tears and smiled. He smiled too.

"I will go and see about the horses," he said, and as she did not answer he left her.

She went back to the flowers. So she had not been able to give them to him. She would throw away the dandelions. As she took them out of the glass, she recalled the words, "You have something real there." They had certainly not been said about the dandelions, but they had often since recurred to her. Was it strange that they should do so now? She let the dandelions remain.

Aarö stayed away a long time, more than an hour, but when he returned he was very cheerful. He was in a smart ladies' sledge, in the handsome furs which he had worn the day before; the most valuable ones that she had ever seen. He saluted with his whip, and talked and laughed with every one, old and young, who gathered round him while Ella put on her things. That was soon done; she had not many wraps, nor did she need them.

He got down when she appeared, came forward, muffled her up and drove off at a trot. As they went he stooped over her and whispered, "How good of you to come with me." His voice was very genial, but there was something quite different about his breath. As soon as the handsome horses had slackened speed, he stooped forward again.

"I have telephoned to Baadshaug to order lunch, it will be ready when we get there; you do not mind?"

She turned, so as to raise her head towards him, their faces almost met.

"I forgot to thank you for the card yesterday."

He coloured. "I repented afterwards," he said, "but at the moment, I could not but think of you; how you suit it out here." Now *she* coloured and drew back. Then she heard close by her: "You must not be angry, it always happens that when we wish to repair a blunder, we make another."

She would have liked to have seen his eyes, as he said this, but she dare not look at him. At all events it was more than he had said up to the present time.

His words fell softly on her ears. Before to-day she had almost misinterpreted his reserve, but how beautiful it made everything. She worshipped it.

"In a little time we shall come to the woods, then we will stop and look round us," he said.

"*There*," she thought.

He drove on at a quick trot. How happy she was! The sunlight sparkled on the snow, the air was warm, she had to loosen the shawl over her head, and he helped her to do so. Again she became aware of his breath, there was something, not tobacco, more delicate, pleasanter, but what was it? It seemed to harmonise with him. She felt very happy, with an overflow of joy in the scene through which they were driving and which continually increased in beauty.

On one side of the road were the mountains, the white mountains, which took a warm tint from the sunlight. In front of the mountains were lower hills, partly covered by woods, and among these lay scattered farms. The farms were soon passed and then came woods, nothing but woods. On the other side of the road they had the sea for the whole way, but between them and it were flat expanses, probably marshes. The sea looked steel-grey against the snow. It spoke of another part of life, of eternal unrest; protest after protest against the snow idyl.

During the thaw, tree-trunks, branches, and fences had become wet. The first snow which fell, being itself wet, had stuck to them. But when all this froze together, and there was another overwhelming fall, outlines were formed over the frozen surface, such as one rarely sees the like of. The weight of the first soft snow had caused it to slip down, but it had been arrested here and there by each inequality, and there it had collected, or else it had slid under the branches, or down on both sides of the fences; when this had been augmented both by drift and fall, the most whimsical animal forms were produced— white cats, white hares clawed the tree-trunks with bent backs and heads and fore-quarters outstretched, or sat under the branches, or on the hedges. White beasts were there, some appeared the size of martens, but occasionally they seemed as large as lynxes or even tigers; besides these there were numberless small animals, white mice, and squirrels, here, there, and everywhere. Again there were, besides, all sorts of oddities, mountebanks who hung by their heels, clowns and goblins on the tops of the fences, dwarfs with big sacks on their backs; an old hat or a nightcap: an animal without a head, another with a neck of preposterous length, an enormous mitten, an overturned water-can. In some places the blackened foliage remained uncovered, and formed arabesques against the drifts; in others, masses of snow lay on the branches of the fir-trees with green above and beneath, forming wonderful contrasts of colour. Aarö drew up and they both got out of the sledge.

Now they gained a whole series of fresh impressions. Right in front of them stood an old pine-tree, half prostrated in the struggle of life; but was he not dreaming, here in the winter, the loveliest of all dreams, that he was young again? In the joyous growth of this snow-white glory he had forgotten all pain and decay, forgotten the moss on his bark, the rottenness of his roots was concealed. A rickety gate had been taken from its place and was propped against the fence, broken and useless. The artist hand of winter had sought it out too, and glorified it, and it was now an architectural masterpiece. The slanting black gate-posts were a couple of young dandies, with hats on one side and jaunty air. The old, grey, mossy rails—one could not imagine Paradise within a more beautiful enclosure. Their blemishes had in this resurrection become their greatest beauty. Their knots and crannies were the chief building ground for the snow, each hole filled up by a donation of heavenly crystals from the clouds. Their disfiguring splinters were now covered and kissed, shrouded and decorated; all blemishes were obliterated in the universal whiteness. A tumbledown moss-grown hut by the roadside— now more extravagantly adorned than the richest bride in the world, covered over from heaven's own lap in such abundance that the white snow wreaths hung half a yard beyond the roof; in some places folded back with consummate art. The grey-black wall under the snow wreaths looked like an old Persian fabric. It seemed ready to appear in a Shakespearean drama. The background of mountains and hills gleamed in the sunlight.

In the midst of all this Ella seemed to hear two little cries of "Mamma, mamma!" When she looked round for her companion he was sitting on the sledge, quite overcome, while tears flowed down his cheeks.

They drove on again, but slowly. "I remember this muddy road," said he; his voice sounded very sad. "The trees shaded it so that it was hardly ever dry, but now it is beautiful."

She turned and raised her head towards him. "Ah! sing a little," she said.

He did not answer at once, and she regretted that she had asked him; at length he said:

"I was thinking of it, but I became so agitated; do not speak for a moment and then perhaps I can—the old winter song, that is to say."

She understood that he could not do so until he completely realised it. These silent enthusiasts were indeed fastidious about what was genuine. Most things were not genuine enough for them. That is why they are so prone to intoxicate themselves; they wish to get away, to form a world for themselves. Yes, now he sang:

In winter's arms doth summer sleep
     By winter covered calm she lay,
     "Still!" he cried to the river's play,
To farm, and field and mountain steep.
     Silence reigns o'er hill and dale,
     No sound at home save ringing flail.

All that summer loved to see
     Till she returns sleeps safely on.
     In needed rest, the summer gone,
Sleep water, meadow-grass and tree,
     Hid like the kernel in the nut
     The earth lies crumbling round each root.

All the ills which summer knew,
     Pest and blight for life and fruit
     Winter's hosts have put to rout.
In peace she shall awake again
     Purified by winds and snows,
     Peace shall greet her as she goes.

A lovely dream has winter strown
     On the sleeping mountain height;
     Star high, pale in northern light,
From sight to sight it bears her on
     Through the long, long hours of night,
     Till she wakes shall be her flight.

He who we say brings naught but pain
     Lives but for that he ne'er shall see.
     He who is called a murderer, he
Preserves each year our land again,
     Then hides himself by crag and hill
     Till evening's breeze again blows chill.

All the little sleigh-bells accompanied the song, like the twitter of sparrows. His voice echoed through the trees, the religious service of a human soul in the white halls.

One day, felt Ella, paid for a thousand. One day may do what the winter song relates. It may rock a weary summer, destroy its germs of ill, renew the earth, make the nerves strong, and the darkest time bright. In it are collected all our long dreams. What might she not have become, poor little thing that she was, if she had had many such days? What would she not then have become, for her children.

They now drew near to a long building with two wings; the whole built of wood. In the courtyard a number of sledges were standing. There were a great many people here then! A stableman took their horses; the waiter who was to attend to them, a German, was quickly at hand, and a bareheaded jovial man joined them as well—it was Peter Klausson. He seemed to have been expecting them, and wished to relieve Ella of her wraps, but he smelt of cognac or something of the sort, and to get rid of him she inquired for the room in which they were to lunch. They were shown into a warm cosy apartment where the table was laid. Aarö helped her off with her things.

"I could not endure Peter Klausson's breath," she said, at which Aarö smiled.

"In America we have a remedy for that."

"What do you mean?"

"One takes something which scents the breath."

A moment later he asked her to excuse him. He had to arrange a few things. She was thus alone until some one knocked at the door. It was Peter Klausson again. He saw her astonishment and smiled.

"We are to lunch together," he said.

"Are we?" she replied.

She looked at the table; it was laid for five.

"Have you heard lately from your husband?"

"No."

A long pause. Was Peter Klausson fit company for Aksel Aarö? Her husband's boon companion! Aarö, who will have nothing but what is genuine. But as she thought this, she had to admit that Peter Klausson's impulsive nature was perfectly truthful, which indeed it was. The waiter came in with a basket of wine, but did not shut the door after him until he had lifted in some more from outside: champagne in ice.

"Shall we want so much wine?" asked Ella.

"Oh, it's all right," answered Peter Klausson, evidently delighted.

"But Aarö does not drink wine!"

"Aarö? When he asked me to come here to-day—I chanced to look in on him —we had some first-rate cognac together."

Ella turned to the window, for she felt that she had grown pale.

Very soon Aarö came in, so courteous and stately that Peter Klausson felt compelled to take his hands out of his pockets. He hardly dared to speak. Aarö said that he had invited the Holmbos, but they had just sent an excuse. They three must make the best of each other's society. He led Ella to the table.

It was soon evident that Aarö was the most delightful and accomplished of hosts. He spoke English to the waiter, and directed him by frequent signs, covered his blunders, and smoothed away every little difficulty, in such a way that it was hardly noticed. All the time he kept up a constant flow of conversation, narrating small anecdotes from his experiences of society, but he never poured out wine for himself, and when he raised his glass his hand shook. Ella had fancied before that this was the case—it was torture to her now.

Oysters were served for the first course; she relished them thoroughly, for she was very hungry; but as the meal proceeded, she became each moment less able to enjoy it. At last her throat seemed to contract, she felt more inclined to cry than to eat and drink.

At first the reason was not clear to her. She only felt that this was absolutely different from what she had dreamed of. This glorious day was to be a disappointment. At first she thought—this will end some time, and we shall go comfortably home again. But by degrees, as his spirits rose, she became merely the guest of a society man. As such she was shown all imaginable attention—indeed, the two gentlemen joined in making much of her, till she could have cried.

After luncheon she was ceremoniously conducted on Aarö's arm into another room which was also in readiness for them; comfortable, well furnished, and with a piano.

Coffee was served at once with liqueur, and not long afterwards the two men asked to be excused; they wanted to smoke, they would not be long. They went, and left her alone. This was scarcely polite, and now she first realised that it was not the day only, but Aarö, who had become different from what she had believed him. The great darkness which had overwhelmed her on the night of the ball again menaced her; she fought against it; she got up and paced the room; she longed to be out of doors, as though she could find him again there, such as she had imagined him. She looked for the luncheon-room, put on her red shawl, and had just come out on to the broad space before the building, when the waiter came up to her and said something in English which she could not at first understand. Indeed, she was too much occupied with her own thoughts to be able suddenly to change languages.

The waiter told her that one of her companions was ill, and the other not to be found. Even when she understood the words, she did not realise what was the matter, but followed mechanically. As she went she remembered that Aarö's tongue had not been quite obedient when, after the liqueur, he had asked permission to go and smoke; surely he had not had a stroke.

They passed the smoking-room, which seemed to be full—at all events of smoke and laughter. The door of a little room by the side of it was opened; there lay Aksel Aarö on a bed. He must have slunk in there alone, perhaps to drink more; indeed, he had taken a short thick bottle in with him, which still stood on a table by the bed, on which he lay fully dressed with closed eyes and without sense or feeling.

"Tip, tip, Peté!" he said to her, and repeated it with outstretched finger, "Tip, tip, Peté!" He spoke in a falsetto voice. Did he mean Peter? Did he take her for a man? Behind him on a pillow lay something hairy; it was a *toupet*; she now saw that he was bald on the crown. "Tip, tip, Peté!" she heard as she rushed out.

Few people have felt smaller than Ella as she trudged along the country road, back to the town as fast as her short legs could carry her, in thin shoes and winter attire. The heavy cloak which she had worn for driving was unfastened, she carried the shawl in her hand, but still the perspiration streamed off her; the idea was upon her that it was her dreams which were falling from her.

At first she only thought of Aksel Aarö, the unhappy lost one! To-morrow or the next day he would leave the country; she knew this from past experience, and this time it would be for ever.

But as she thought how terrible it was, the *toupet* on the pillow seemed to ask: "Was Aksel Aarö so very genuine?" "Yes, yes, how could he help it if he became bald so early." "H'm," answered the *toupet*; "he could have confessed to it."

She struggled on; luckily she did not meet any one, nor was she overtaken by any of those who had been at Baadshaug. She must look very comical, perspiring and tearful, with unfastened cloak, in thin shoes and with a shawl in her hand. Several times she slackened her pace, but the disturbance of her feelings was too great, and it was her nature to struggle forward.

But through all her feverish haste the great question forced itself upon her: "Would you not wish now, Ella, to relinquish all your dreams, since time after time things go so badly?" She sobbed violently and answered: "Not for worlds. No! for these dreams are the best things that I have. They have given me the power to measure others so that I can never exalt anything which is base. No! I have woven them round my children as well, so that I have a thousand times more pleasure in them. They and the flowers are all that I have." And she sobbed and pressed on.

"But now you will have no dream, Ella!"

At first she did not know what to reply to this, it seemed but too true, too terribly true, and the *toupet* showed itself again.

It was here that Aarö had sung the old winter song, and as the tinkle of the sledge-bells had accompanied it, so now her tears were unceasingly accompanied by two little voices: "Mamma, mamma!" It was not strange, for it was towards the children that she was hurrying, but now they seemed to demand that she should dream about them. No, no! "You have something real there," Aarö's voice seemed to say. She remembered his saying it, she remembered his sadness as he did so. Had he really thought of himself and her, or of the children and her? Had he compared his own weakness with their health, with their future? Her thoughts wandered far away from the boys, and she was once more immersed in all his words and looks, trying by them to solve this enigma. But these, with the yearning and pain, came back as they had never done before. Her whole life was over; her dream was of too long standing, too strong, too clear, the roots could not be pulled up; it was impossible. Were they not round everything which, next day, she should see, or touch, or use? As a last stroke she remembered that the boys were not at home; she would come to an empty house.

But she resisted still; for when she got home and had bathed and gone to bed, and again the moonlight shone in on her and reminded her of her thoughts the night before, she turned away and cried aloud like a child. None could enter, none could hear her; her heart was young, as though she were but seventeen; it could not, it would not give up!

What was it, in fact, that she had wished for to-day? She did not know—no, she did not! She only knew that her happiness was *there*—and so she had let it remain. Now she was disappointed and deluded in a way that certainly few had been.

She could not bear to desecrate him further. Then the winter song swept past in his voice, sweet, full, sorrowful, as if it wished to make all clear to her; and, tractable as a child, she composed herself and listened. What did it say? That her dreams united two summers, the one which had been and the one which was slowly struggling up anew. Thanks be to the dreams which had awakened it. It said, too, that the dreams were something in themselves often of greater truth than reality itself. She had felt this when she was tending her flowers.

In her uneasy tossing in her bed, her plait had come close to her hand. Sadly she drew it forward; he had kissed it again to-day. And so she lay on her side, and took it between her hands, and cried.

"Mamma, mamma!" she heard whispered, and thus she slept.

Ingram Content Group UK Ltd.
Milton Keynes UK
UKHW011944270323
419267UK00003B/44